DECADENT
MASTER

Also by Tawny Taylor:

Wicked Beast

Dark Master

Real Vamps Don't Drink O-Neg

Sex and the Single Ghost

DECADENT MASTER

TAWNY TAYLOR

APHRODISIA

KENSINGTON BOOKS

http://www.kensingtonbooks.com

APHRODISIA BOOKS are published by

Kensington Publishing Corp.
119 West 40th Street
New York, NY 10018

ISBN-13: 978-0-7582-4695-0
ISBN-10: 0-7582-4695-1

First Kensington Trade Paperback Printing: March 2010

10 9 8 7 6 5 4 3 2 1

Printed in the United States of America

DECADENT MASTER

1

Well, damn. His days of hedonistic excess were coming to an end, at least temporarily. But if Dierk Sorenson had anything to say about it, he'd be back to his overindulgent ways in no time.

"There he is!" his brother Rolf exclaimed, as Dierk opened the front door of the family's newest real estate acquisition, a six-thousand-square-foot house in Franklin Village. The building sat far back from the road, on a sloping, wooded lot. Two acres. Private. Quiet. It was perfect. Of course, if the neighbors had any idea their newest arrival was a pack of vampires, they might not agree. "Our prodigal son has returned."

"I'm not your son," Dierk remarked, shoving past his jeering brother as he stepped through the door. "And I'm not here to stay. Where's our formidable king, Shadow?"

"In the library, I think. Hey, aren't you going to give your baby brother a hug?"

"No." Dierk sensed his irritating brother was tailing him, like he used to when they were younger. Some things never changed.

The nauseating scent of fresh paint burned his nostrils, just another of a long list of minor annoyances Dierk had to deal with today. Dammit, a ripe woman was all he wanted right now. None of this shit.

He found Shadow in the library, as Rolf had suggested, along with another brother, Stefan.

Shadow glanced up from the paperwork strewn across his desk, giving Dierk a cautious smile. "Glad to see you could make it."

"I always respond to a summons from my king," Dierk responded coolly.

Stefan left his post next to Shadow to give Dierk a clap on the back. "It's good to see you, brother."

"Yeah, you, too." Dierk scowled.

"Don't be so enthusiastic, bro. Shadow might decide to keep you around permanently." They exchanged glances and then Dierk busted into a hearty guffaw and yanked his brother into a tight hug. "Good to see you, too."

Franklin, Michigan, might not be his favorite place on earth, but it was great seeing his brothers again. It had been over a year. Damn, how time flew when you were hiding from your demons.

Shadow cleared his throat, reminding the brothers that he'd had a reason for dragging Dierk to this dull little corner of suburbia. "Leave us. We need to talk. In private."

"Later," Stefan said, giving Dierk one last grin.

"How about we head to the bar later?" Rolf offered.

"Yeah, sure," Dierk said. Metro Detroit's night life wasn't anything like that of New York, Paris, or Amsterdam, but in a pinch it would do. Dierk had seen worse. At Shadow's invitation, he sat in a chair next to the fireplace. Shadow took the matched mate sitting next to his. "So, what's the proposal you wanted to run past me?" Dierk asked.

"It's not so much a proposal as it is a favor."

"Yeah? A favor from me? I'm not the most reliable of the

twelve of us, in case you hadn't noticed." He was damn proud of his reputation as the black sheep of the family. He lived for the next sin, the next indulgence, the next corruption.

"I have. But this is something I think you are particularly suited for. I need someone to run Twilight for me."

Dierk groaned. "Your bondage club? You sent your private jet—dragged me halfway across the globe—to ask me to run your little bondage club? Anyone can manage that place—"

"That's not necessarily true." Shadow's expression darkened. "There've been some . . . problems there lately. Nothing major—"

"You don't need me. You're full of shit."

Shadow wasn't bothered in the least by his younger brother calling his bluff. "Maybe. Okay, yes I am. Not about needing someone to run the club, just the reason why."

Dierk shook his head, seeing where this was going. He didn't like strolling into a trap, but that was exactly what he was doing. Eyes wide open. "You should shut that money pit down. You're always complaining about it running in the red. Why keep sinking money into it?"

"Because it's the only bondage club in southeast Michigan. And, more important, it's the only one in the state for *our kind*."

"So, they can drive up to Lansing. It's only an hour-and-a-half drive. Besides, who says 'our kind' can't play side by side with mortals? You ask me, and I'll tell you that a human slave boy is just as much fun as an immortal one. You just have to be a little careful, that's all. Can't get carried away with the restraints, since they need to breathe. Then again, we all know that, since we've all played with mortal women."

His brother, notorious for having the determination of a mule, shook his head. "I have my reasons for not closing the place down, the primary one being it's my way of showing our people that I do care about their daily needs. An hour-and-a-half drive one way is not exactly convenient." Shadow stood, walked around his desk, and lowered himself into the high-back leather chair. "Not that I should have to explain any of this to you. Either you'll agree to run the place, at least until I find someone to take over permanently, or you won't. What'll it be?"

"Are you saying this gig is temporary?" He was a fool. "How long do you think it'll take you to find someone else?" A complete and utter idiot.

"Can't say. Hiring your replacement isn't high on my priority list." His brother snatched up a piece of paper and stared down at it for a few beats before glancing up. "I'm not going to lie to try to convince you to help me out." Dierk just about laughed in his brother's face at that one. "I've hired several general managers outside of the family, and they've all been disasters. This has to stay in the family, and every other Sorenson male, even Rolf, has turned down the position."

"The place is that bad?"

"No, it's no better or worse than any other bondage club you've been to." Shadow went back to reading the paper he was holding.

What would he do now? Dierk knew he was being lured into a trap, but damn if he knew what kind of trap it was. None of what his brother was saying made any sense. And this was the last thing he wanted, to be chained to a failing bondage club for the next year or more.

He stood, walked to an overloaded shelf, and ran an index finger down the spine of a dusty old book. He pulled the volume off and flipped the pages. "Then why'd all of our brothers turn it down? Every one of us is a Dom. We all practice the lifestyle, in one form or another. It's in our blood."

"Yeah, I know." Shadow snatched up a pen and started scrawling in his jerky handwriting on the page now lying flat on his desk. "But it seems the others might like to hang out at

Twilight in their free time. They don't want to make it a career."

Dierk dropped the book on Shadow's desk. It landed with a dull thud. He planted his hands on the glossy top and leaned forward, glaring. "That's the shittiest nonexplanation I've ever heard."

Shadow shrugged. "You've always been a straight shooter, little brother. I knew that wouldn't change, even when you're talking to your *king.* . . ."

That was true. His mouth might've gotten him in trouble a time or two, but at least no one could ever say that he was a bullshitter.

". . . and the brother who has helped you out of a scrape or two before," Shadow added.

Shit. Dierk straightened up. His brother was going to play *that* card. "I'll give you a month."

"Twelve."

"Six, and that's my final offer."

"Done." Shadow thrust his hand out, reaching across his desk. "You can start tomorrow night. Rolf will show you around."

Dierk shook his brother's hand, knowing without a doubt that he'd just taken the bait. What kind of hell had he just walked into?

Shadow released his hand. "I hope you'll consider living here, with us."

He smiled as he took in the shelves weighed down with books, the furniture and artwork, the huge wall of windows stretching the entire length of the room. At the moment, the drapes were pulled back, revealing the lush landscaping outside. Silver moonlight shimmered in the raindrops clinging to the leaves of the lilac bushes, now in full bloom, giving the whole place an ethereal otherworldly glow. It was damn . . . pretty. "No, I don't think I'd fit in here. This place is too cheery for my taste. I'll find a cozy little hovel closer to work, if that's okay with you." At his brother's assent, he left the library, in search of Rolf. It was still early. He didn't have to be anywhere until tomorrow night. It was time to let loose and release some tension.

There was plenty of trouble he could get himself into in the next twenty hours. He was determined to make sure some of that trouble involved alcohol and a lush woman who was willing to sate his needs. It had been too long, at least forty-eight hours, since he'd heard a sub beg for mercy.

It sucked, being a man of honor. The last thing in the world he wanted, or needed, was a regular full-time job. But thanks to his inability to deny his brother any favor he asked, that was exactly what he'd just gotten. Worse yet, he had no doubt there was more to this gig than his brother was letting on.

"Take me somewhere where the bourbon runs like a river and the women are easy," he said by way of a greeting when he found Rolf in the living room, sprawled across a couch, watching a football game.

Rolf twisted his upper body, glancing over his shoulder at him. "I have the perfect spot in mind. Want to freshen up or anything first?"

"No. I'm as fresh as I'm going to get. Let's go." He tipped his head toward the front foyer, then, not waiting for Rolf, he turned and headed that way. It had been a helluva long flight from Amsterdam. He needed to unwind.

"Hey, where're you going?" Stefan asked, coming down the circular front stairs. Wearing his usual, neatly pressed black pants and shirt, he was looking a little overdressed for the kind of bar Dierk favored.

"Just heading out for a drink or two," Rolf answered from behind Dierk. "Wanna come?"

"Yeah. It's been a while since I let loose."

"Just don't embarrass me, you two," Dierk tossed over his shoulder as he pulled open the front door. "If one of you sings karaoke, I'm outta there."

"Damn," Stefan cussed, laughter in his voice. "Bailey's is having their grand championship contest tonight. I can do a mean Barry Manilow."

"Oh yeah, 'Copacabana' is one of my favorites," Rolf said, nodding his head. "Although I'd rather go for 'Every Breath You Take' by the Police. I've been told I have a gritty voice, like Sting."

Laughing, Dierk headed outside, shuddering not because it was cold, but because of the horror of imagining Rolf belting out a Police tune. The man was tone deaf. "No, no, no. I'm not listening to a bunch of wannabes bellow eighties tunes. Not a chance."

He shared an easy camaraderie with his brothers as he rode shotgun in Rolf's car. They avoided talking about the worst of the events of the past year: the destruction of their childhood home in Eastern Europe and the shocking and devastating loss of their only sister, Tyra.

Instead, Rolf and Stefan took turns telling him war stories of the women they'd conquered and the ones that had gotten away. And, for just a split second or two, Dierk almost regretted missing some of those nights.

Some twenty minutes later, they pulled into a parking lot snugged against the side of a red brick building. A flickering neon sign announced BOB'S BAR. A line of Harleys hugged the side of the building.

Felt like home.

The building's dark interior was thick with cigarette smoke, the music loud, the women hot, ready . . . and willing. A pair of leggy blondes with full lips, tits that made his cock hard, and asses that begged to be spanked gave him a once-over.

Yep, he was home.

He eased himself onto a barstool, ordered a double, and invited the blondes to join him with a nod of the head.

Wynne Fischer leaned back against the couch and closed her eyes. It was so much easier talking about this subject—about sex—with her eyes closed. No matter who she was talking with, male or female, friend or counselor, sex was just one of those subjects she had a really hard time discussing. "The little things are what get me going. A soft touch on the small of my back. A wicked grin when no one else is looking. A sexy note left in an unexpected place." She sighed. "I don't understand. Why would anyone need all that other stuff—whips and chains? It's just not sexy. Or loving."

Her therapist, Susan Smith, took a moment before responding, "How does it make you feel, learning that your fiancé found those things sexy?"

"How do you think?" Wynne blinked open her eyes for the sole purpose of rolling them. God, this counselor was already starting to sound like the last one, and the one before that. Did they all share the same script or something? Where could a girl go to get some *real* help? "Confused."

"Anything else? How did you feel after learning he was gay, on top of everything else?"

"I don't know." She closed her eyes again and let her mind go back to that awful day, which hadn't started awful at all. It had been a pretty April day. The air smelled really good, like grass and earth. The sun was warm. They were walking in the park, talking about the last minute details of their wedding plans. The puppy they'd just adopted was scampering around their ankles, nipping at their shoelaces.

John had been quiet lately, and she had been worried about him. She kept prodding him to tell her what was bothering him, until he'd finally confessed everything, there in the park, next to the jungle gym. He admitted he was having an affair with one of his coworkers—a guy—and had been living a secret life for almost two years.

Her life didn't just fall apart. It blew up in her face.

"I guess I felt empty inside," she confessed. "Numb, at least for a while."

"What about now? Do you still feel empty and numb?"

"No. Now I'm confused, wondering if I did something wrong . . . to make him turn to men. I'm hurt that he kept so many secrets from me. Shocked he did so for so long. I didn't have a clue." She met Susan's brown-eyed gaze. "I honestly thought we were happy. How could I not know things were so wrong? Am I that oblivious? That blind?"

The counselor gave Wynne an encouraging smile. "Of course not. You wanted to believe the best. I think that's human nature. Your fiancé never gave you any reason to think anything was seriously wrong."

"Yes, you're right. He misled me." As Wynne bent over and picked up her purse, she felt a new emotion drift to the surface. Her face warmed. Her heart started thumping heavily in her chest. "He lied. For months and months. We had sex. Lots of sex. He acted like he enjoyed it. *Pretended* it was good."

"And that makes you feel . . . ?"

"Maybe a little mad."

"A little?" Susan leaned forward. "Wynne, you don't need permission to feel any emotion. It's okay."

Wynne nodded, jerking on her purse's zipper. "Okay, maybe I'm more than a *little* mad. Maybe I'm very mad, pissed . . . furious. Absolutely livid. It wasn't fair for him to let things drag on so long if he wasn't happy." Finding a pack of gum, she snatched a piece, unwrapped it, wadded the wrapper up, and stuffed the stick into her mouth. She chewed so hard her jaw snapped. "We were together for three years. We were engaged for one. And none of this came up until a few weeks before our wedding."

She swiped at the hot tears streaming from her eyes, tugging a tissue from the box Susan handed her. "It wasn't fair to keep such important secrets from me. I mean, maybe John knew I wouldn't understand that whole whips and chains thing. That could be part of the reason why he kept it quiet. And the gay part . . . oh God. But still. It's just wrong, what he did." She closed her purse and set it on the floor. "Then again, I keep telling myself he probably couldn't help it. He was probably ashamed. Suffering."

"What do you mean, 'couldn't help it'?"

"I've been doing some reading about sex addiction. How people get sucked into depravity, needing harder and harder stimulation. It wasn't John's fault, I don't think. He was . . . sick. Right? That's what I have to keep telling myself." Noticing Susan was staring at her hands, she glanced down. She'd torn the tissue to shreds without realizing it. She raked the ripped bits into a pile and balled them up, stuffing them into her pocket. "It's the only way I can deal with this without going absolutely crazy. I mean, what else could it be? It has to be a sickness, right? An addiction. Normal sex with a woman simply wasn't enough anymore."

Susan didn't respond for a long time, which drove Wynne absolutely nuts. Finally, she said, "First, from a purely professional standpoint, to say all people who participate in bondage or are gay are 'sick' is not a fair—"

Something hot and furious exploded inside her. "Fair? Who the hell cares about fair?" Wynne pulled another tissue from the box and dabbed at her watery eyes. "John didn't think about what was fair. And his gay fuck partner didn't either. If they did, we would be married right now, buying our first house together, planning to start a family. Because he told me that was what was going to happen. He'd promised me. Like you said, any emotion I'm feeling is good. Right? So you can't fault me for hating the culture or lifestyle or whatever you call it that took my John away. My life. My dreams."

Susan seemed to be trying to hide a frown. "I hear a lot of anger in those words."

"Yeah, I'm sure you do. I just don't get it. Why would any man leave a woman who loves him with all her heart for someone who beats him? Why? Why would he suddenly decide sex with me was so bad that he needed to quit having sex with women forever? If he didn't go homosexual because of an addiction then I *turned* the man gay. How'd I manage that? Please, please tell me." She held her breath, waiting, hoping for the words that would make this whole thing make sense. That's all she wanted, for someone to say the right thing, so that the lightbulb would come on, she would understand, and she'd finally be out of this dark hell.

"I think we've got our work cut out for us. For one thing, you need to understand that you did nothing wrong. John didn't 'turn' gay. He was gay all along. And second, you don't know what bondage is about. Until you do, you're not going to put this behind you. Do you agree?" At Wynne's shrug, the therapist added, "I don't want you to continue to doubt yourself, your sexuality, your ability to trust, to love. Which is why I want to make a suggestion."

Damn, there'd been no lightbulb moment. "What kind of suggestion?"

"I wonder." Susan paused for a moment, visibly contemplating something. "Would you consider a little exercise? I think it might help you find the answers you're looking for."

"I guess that depends upon the 'exercise' you're suggesting. If it means I'll finally get over this crap, so I can find a man who can love me and not scare him away with my paranoia, then maybe I'm desperate enough to try just about anything."

"I want you to go to a bondage club."

Wynne barked out a laugh. Her stomach almost came out with it. "You're kidding, right?"

"No, I'm not."

"Then maybe you're the one who needs a shrink. Not me. Because that's just . . . wrong."

Susan pursed her lips, shaking her head. "There's that sarcasm again. Remember, use *feeling* words."

Argh! "Okay, I *feel* like you're the one who needs a shrink. That's the most insane idea I have ever heard."

"And why do you think it's crazy?"

"Because you're sending me into *that* world. With people I don't understand . . . What could I possibly gain by going to a bondage club?"

"Honestly, there's a very good reason why I think paying a visit to a bondage club is a good idea. But I won't force you. It's your choice."

"Then I choose not to."

"Very well, then. If you aren't willing to do this for yourself, you wouldn't have gained any useful insight by going anyway, only ammunition for prejudice and hatred." Susan looked weary as she glanced at the clock. "Our time is up. We'll talk again in two weeks. But before you go, I want to give you the phone number of someone I trust very much. In case you change your mind. She can get you into the local bondage club, Twilight. It's very safe and exclusive." She scrawled a name on the back of one of her cards and offered it to Wynne.

"All right." Wynne reluctantly accepted the proffered card and stuffed it into her pocket with the torn-up tissue. She stood, gave Susan-the-crazy-shrink a friendly wave, and headed out of the office. She found her friend Kristy sitting in the waiting room, her head buried in a romance novel. Wynne gave her a tap on the shoulder and headed for the exit.

"I'm guessing you don't like your new therapist very much?" her intuitive friend asked as they walked to the car.

"You guessed right."

"What is it this time?" Kristy ducked into the passenger seat before adding, "This is the third counselor you've ditched in six months. You know, maybe it's not them—"

"That woman suggested I go to a bondage club." Wynne tossed the business card onto the dash, crammed the key into the ignition, and gave it a jerk.

"Why would she do that?" her friend asked, plucking up the card to read it.

"Because she's cuckoo, that's why." Wynne rammed the gear shift into drive and stomped on the gas, sending the car lurching out of the parking space.

Wow, she could see herself overreacting, but she couldn't stop. Her heart wasn't just pounding in her chest, it was jackhammering. Her skin wasn't just hot, it was blistering. And this awful, overwhelming twitchy rage was rushing through her body, relentless and overpowering.

Kristy thrust her arms forward, grabbing the dash. "Maybe I'd better drive."

"No." Wynne took a few deep breaths. "I'm sorry. I won't drive like an ass. I promise. This isn't worth killing anyone over."

Kristy waited a while, several minutes, and finally, after she must have been convinced Wynne had pulled herself together, she asked, "Okay, so why did your new therapist say she wanted you to go to a bondage dungeon?"

"Because she thinks I won't get over this thing with John until I understand bondage. I think it bothered her a little when I suggested people who do that stuff were abnormal for wanting to be beaten."

Kristy gaped. "You said that?"

"Yeah. Kind of." After seeing Kristy's reaction, Wynne started second-guessing herself. "Um, I said something like they have a sex addiction and can't help themselves."

"Your counselor has a point, then. That's a judgmental thing to say."

"Yeah, maybe." When a glance at her friend's face left her feeling like crap, she added, "I was upset, you know? She kept pushing me to tell her how I felt, so I did. I wasn't thinking. The words just came out. Even if I don't believe everyone who goes to bondage dungeons is a sick addict, it doesn't change anything. I won't go to one of those places." She paused. "I . . . can't."

"Why not? What are you afraid of?"

More silence. "Because those places are creepy. And scary . . . and I just can't." There came the tears again. She blinked to keep her vision clear. Damn it, she hated crying. Hated crying almost as much as she hated feeling like this—like her insides were still as raw as they'd been that day in April.

"Oh, honey. I wish there was something I could do or say to help you through this. I . . . could go with you, if that would make it easier."

"But I don't want to go." Sniffling, she dug in the center console between the seats, looking for another tissue. She found a crumpled McDonald's napkin. "It's not going to change anything. John isn't going to come back to me. So what's the point?"

A long silence stretched between them, broken only by the pathetic sound of Wynne's sniffling.

Kristy sighed. "Maybe Susan Smith, Certified Therapist, knows something we don't. You've tried to get over this thing on your own and it hasn't worked. You've tried two other counselors, and they didn't help either. I say you trust the shrink you're paying God only knows how much and do what she says. You might come out of this understanding why John lied, why he had to leave you. . . . It's been a year," her friend reminded her gently. "You dated one guy since John left, and that lasted for less than a month. Sweetie, you acted like a clingy leech and scared him off. Since then it seems like you've given up. You don't go out anymore. The funny, friendly, easy-going girl I knew is gone."

"Maybe I don't need to be that girl anymore. Maybe she was easygoing because she didn't have a freaking clue what a mess her life was." Wynne hit the power button on the radio, putting an end to the conversation. No denying, it was rude, cutting off her friend like that, but she was pushing too hard and Wynne wasn't in any condition to listen to more psychobabble shit.

Absolutely, she wanted to get out of this hell she'd fallen into. She could step outside of herself, watch herself being a bitch. It was her way of dealing with her pain and anger.

Obviously, despite what all the counselors had said, there was no cure for a broken heart. It would take time. A lot longer than one year. Maybe this girl was a slower-than-average healer.

She just wished someone understood how she felt. Really and truly knew what it felt like to have the one human being on the face of the earth who cared about her turn around and tell her it was all a lie, that he didn't really love her, had maybe never loved her at all. She had a feeling if she ever did find a person who empathized with that kind of pain, they'd be friends forever. Or better yet, more than friends.

"Pull the car over," Kristy said abruptly.

"Why? What's wrong? Are you sick or something?"

"No, just do it. Please."

Wynne looked over her shoulder and eased into the right lane. Then, at the first driveway, an entry to a Burger King, she turned out of traffic and parked.

Kristy cut off the radio. "There's something I need to tell you, and well, this is just as good a time as any. If I keep waiting for the perfect opportunity, I won't ever tell you."

Wynne's heart stopped. A split second later, it kicked back to life, but at a pace that was at least twice its normal rate. "What's wrong? Are you pregnant?"

Kristy rolled her eyes. "No, I'm not pregnant. I get the

Depo shot every three months, like clockwork. How could I be?"

"Well, I don't know. You've been acting a little moody the past few weeks and the shot isn't 100 percent reliable. . . ."

"That's because I've been dealing with some things, too. And I wanted to tell you, but I didn't know how to bring it up. Especially with how you've been feeling lately. But I can't sit here and pretend any longer."

"Pretend what? That you're my friend?"

"No, I'll always be your friend, at least if you want me to be." Kristy glanced away, staring down at her hands.

What did that mean? "Oh for Chrissakes! What's wrong?"

"It's not really that something's wrong. It's just that . . . well, in the last year or so I've come to the realization that . . . I'm . . . gay."

Huh? "You're what?"

Kristy nodded. "I am attracted to women. Sexually."

"I can't believe this. Are you sure?"

Kristy gave her a mean-eyed glare. "Yes, of course I'm sure."

"But you were married. To a man. For years. You have had sex with men. Lots of men—"

Kristy smacked her shoulder. "Hey, not that many!"

"And you're like . . . in your thirties. How could you be gay all of a sudden?" When Kristy didn't offer up an answer to that question, Wynne asked, "What is going on? First John decides he's gay and now you? Why is everyone turning homosexual on me? Let me see that book you were reading. . . ." Wynne snatched the novel off her supposedly gay friend's lap. The cover boasted a typical romance nekkid man titty. The title: *The Barbarian.* "See? You're not gay. You're reading a romance novel. . . ." She flipped the book over and read the blurb. "What is this? It's about two guys? You're reading a gay romance?"

Kristy grabbed her book and dropped it into her enormous purse. "I knew you'd have a hard time with this. Listen, we can talk about my choice in reading material later. This is important. I'm trying to tell you that I have been homosexual—or rather, bisexual—for a long time. I just didn't want to accept it."

"I don't want to accept it either. I mean, we live together. We've slept together. In the same bed. Before your bedroom set was delivered."

"Yeah, I know."

Wynne felt the color draining from her face. "Did you . . . get aroused?"

"No," her friend answered sheepishly. "We're friends. That's all."

"But you're gay."

"Yes."

"You like women."

"Yes."

"And you needed to tell me this now? Today?" Wynne folded a napkin and dragged it under her bottom eyelashes, removing a black smudge of molten eye makeup.

"I know the timing sucks, but I couldn't wait any longer. I'm dating someone. Things are getting serious between us. You were going to figure it out. I mean, how do I explain why I'm taking a woman into my bedroom?"

Wynne glanced at Kristy for a split second then turned to stare out her window. She just couldn't look her friend in the eye right now. She was confused. Overwhelmed. "I don't understand this."

"There's more."

"I don't think I can handle more right now."

"I'm sorry, I really am. But I need to get this last bit off my chest, and then you can take me home and . . . think about stuff, scream, cry, whatever. Okay?"

"God, how bad is this going to be?"

"I've been to the bondage club your therapist recommended. In fact, I'm a member of Twilight. Although everyone there knows me as Mistress Raven. I, uh, wear a wig."

Mistress Raven?

That was it. Wynne's life had just moved from hellacious to bizarre. What was going to happen next? Were aliens going to abduct her? Was the world going to be struck by a giant meteor? Was her father going to call her after twenty-some years and tell her he loved her?

"Do you think I'm a sex addict?" Kristy asked.

God, Wynne wanted to just crawl in a hole now. "No. Like I said, I was just upset—"

"Do you think I'm sick because I like to dominate men and women? Play bondage games?"

"No, of course not. We've known each other since we were in diapers. I know you're not sick."

"Good. Now that we've settled that, I'm going to ask you a favor." Kristy gave her a cat-that-ate-the-canary smile, which made Wynne's insides twist into a knot. "As your best friend. Come with me to the club. One time. Do it for me."

"Kristy, I can't. I just . . . ohmygod. This is a lot to take in all at once." Wynne dropped her head, resting her forehead against the steering wheel.

"Sure it is. We'll talk more about it later. After you've had some time to recover." Kristy patted Wynne's knee, just like she had a million times before. But this time Wynne's body stiffened. Seeming to sense Wynne's reaction, Kristy lifted her hand. "I'm not going to stop nagging you until you agree to go. . . ."

"But—"

"You won't have to do anything. Just watch, talk to some people. . . ."

"Kristy, I can't—"

"... and we can make up some kind of story to tell people so you're not embarrassed."

"That's not the problem. I mean, it is, sort of—"

"It's for your own good. I think your therapist is right."

Dammit, she was going to lose this battle of wills, like she always did. When necessary, Kristy could be a real bulldog. The girl was also an accomplished manipulator.

"You're going to make me beg, aren't you?" Kristy gave a martyred sigh. "You don't love me anymore."

Dammit, if only she didn't love her lesbian-bondage-mistress-manipulating best friend so freaking much. Wynne rocked her head to the side, sending Kristy some sad eyes. "Stop. Please."

"I'm not going to stop until you agree to go. Just once. For me. I want you to get past this, and I need you to understand me, too. Until you do, things are going to be weird between us. You know that, right?"

So much for the sad eyes. Wynne inhaled. Exhaled. She'd needed that oxygen. Her head felt a little clearer. "Fine, fine. But give me a while to prepare. A month or two."

"A week."

"Two weeks."

"Done."

Oh God.

2

"Rumors are that Master Zane has broken the club's rules several times, leading to at least one submissive seeking medical care for injuries," Rolf said as he led Dierk on a quick tour of the club. He stopped inside the main dungeon, kicked a booted foot up onto a bench. "Since I wasn't here at the time, I can't verify or dispute the rumor."

"I'll have to keep an eye on him. Do we keep pictures of our members?"

"Yes, they're kept in our computer. The receptionist out front checks every person in, and if she doesn't personally know them, she checks the picture in the system."

"Good. I'll take a look at the photos when we get back to the office."

"He's easy to pick out in a crowd. He's a dark sonofabitch, with straight black hair. Pulls it back in a ponytail. His eyes are the color of coal, and his mouth is always twisted in a sneer. Looks mean and has a reputation to match. Some members tell me the guy's trouble. Personally, I haven't had any problems with him. I'll tell you this: the submissives, especially the humans, can't seem to resist him, despite his rep for ignoring limits."

Dierk shook his head. That he would not tolerate, especially if the guy had actually injured a submissive he'd been playing with. No Dom had the right to ignore a submissive's limits, ever. Especially when it came to an issue of safety. Every Dom worth a damn knew a submissive's safety was his responsibility.

Safe. Sane. Consensual. Those were the three pillars of their world. If any one of those three were knocked down, the whole damn thing would come crashing to the ground.

What the hell was the guy thinking?

Dierk's nerves were twitchy as he checked the equipment, making sure it had all been maintained properly, cleaned, and sanitized. Meanwhile, Rolf continued his monologue about each member of the club, ending with a human Domme who called herself Mistress Raven.

Dierk glanced at the clock before he checked the last piece of equipment. Ten minutes and it would be sundown. The club would open. And this room would be full of humans and immortals, tops and bottoms, stripping away their everyday identities to become the Master, slave, Dom, or submissive of their fantasy.

Rolf rested an elbow on a nearby support. "The private suites are leased by a handful of members, including Master Zane, who has the last room on the right."

"Do we have keys?" Dierk asked, standing. Everything looked good. Nothing broken or needing repair.

"Sure." Rolf cocked his head to the side. "They're in the office, bottom desk drawer."

"I want to take a look at his suite before he comes in tonight."

"Good idea."

Dierk headed toward the office, his brother trailing close behind. "What about cameras?" Dierk asked.

"We don't have any in the private suites, if that's what you mean."

"I want some installed tomorrow. But I don't want the members to know. I don't trust anyone else to handle this but you. Will you find someone to come in and install them for me? We need a mortal company who can be here before sunset."

"Will do."

"Thanks." Dierk unlocked the desk drawer, snatched up a ring loaded with keys, and headed toward the private suites. "You ever watch the sonofabitch play? Is he intentionally ignoring his submissives' limits or is he just getting carried away?"

"Hard to say. Like I said, the guy looks like he would take on a demon without thinking twice about it. Hell, he might be a demon, for all we know. He's immortal, but I can't say for sure what species. But, as mean as he looks, I've never seen him get outta line."

Dierk unlocked the door and stepped inside. Behind him, Rolf snapped on the lights. A quick look around, and Dierk had the guy summed up. Hardcore sadist. Among his toys, Master Zane had a large and wide assortment of torture instruments, more than he'd seen in one place before. There was the standard—ropes, floggers, paddles, masks, and leather restraints—as well as needles, nails, enemas, equipment for electro play, mummification, and water torture. This was not a Dom for a new bottom. His taste ran to the extreme side of S and M.

Dierk was no angel, had in fact tried most of those activities at least once. Some of them he'd liked. Others, not at all. But even he had some limits on what he'd do in a dungeon.

As the club owner, Dierk couldn't limit the activities that

went on in this room, as long as those three pillars were maintained. Safe. Sane. Consensual. But he would watch this guy closely, and if he stepped even a toe over the line, he'd be out. No explanations. No second chances.

"We better get going," Rolf said, moving toward the door. "Alicia the receptionist will be coming in any minute now. We don't want Zane to know we've been in here."

"Yeah." Dierk followed Rolf out, locking the door behind them. He pocketed the keys just as he heard the back door chime.

He shared a knowing smile with his brother and headed toward his office to view the digital picture files. Rolf went to gather the employees as they arrived.

After a quick introduction to the staff, Dierk gave a short speech about making sure their guests were safe at all times. Then he sent them off to see to their jobs.

The club wasn't just a bondage dungeon. There was also a bar and restaurant in the building, catering to a more mainstream human crowd, which meant there were over fifty people to manage, including cooks, waiters and waitresses, bartenders, dishwashers, and maintenance crew. Human and immortal, both.

If there was one thing he hated, it was having someone looking over his back, telling him how to do his job. He wasn't going to be that kind of boss to his staff.

His staff. Damn, that sounded strange.

After the impromptu meeting, Dierk settled himself at the small nonalcoholic bar positioned at the front of the dungeon and ordered a yerba mate. He swiveled his stool around to watch the action unfolding behind him, in the dungeon. His eyes meandered through the room, from a Shibari scene just beginning in the corner, to a Mistress training a lovely little olive-complexioned slave girl on a kneeler, to the entry, where a pair of women had just stepped into the room.

The one on the right he recognized from his quick perusal of the photographs on file. Mistress Raven. The one on the left, however, was new.

"Looks like Mistress Raven brought in some fresh meat," Rolf said, taking the seat beside him.

Dierk grabbed his cup, taking a sip of the grassy-flavored hot beverage. Humans drank it for its health benefits. He drank it to clear his mind. An immortal didn't need anything to counteract cellular destruction or improve his immune system.

Rolf sighed. "What a sweet little thing she is," he mused. "Obviously scared out of her mind."

"Yeah," Dierk agreed, tracking the petite brunette as she followed her hostess, almond-shaped eyes wide, little heart-shaped face pale. Her lush lips, coated with a layer of deep pink lipstick, were slightly parted in a sexy pout. He suddenly ached to kiss that pink lipstick off, smear it all over her sweet face.

"My money's on that one leaving before the half hour's up," Rolf said, extending a hand. "What do you say? Wanna bet me . . . a thousand?"

"I say you're not very sure of yourself if that's all you're willing to lay on the table." Dierk gave his brother's hand a shake, hoping Rolf was wrong, and not because he'd lose the money. It had been a long time since he'd watched an innocent get broken in. There was no greater rush than watching the training of a new bottom.

The brunette's hostess waved in their direction and Dierk glanced back, realizing she was signaling Rolf. Clearly, his brother hadn't been exaggerating when he'd said he spent a lot of time in the club—which begged the question of why he'd turned down the offer to run the place.

Dierk made a mental note to ask him later.

"She's heading this way," Rolf stated the obvious. "Maybe she's looking for a Dom for her friend."

"And I'm the man on the moon," Dierk said, noting the newbie's tight expression. She wasn't nervous like the average new submissive was. There wasn't a speck of curiosity in those deep mocha-hued eyes of hers. Only fear, mixed with a little . . . hostility?

Interesting. What was her story? Dierk couldn't wait to hear it.

Wynne had never been so petrified.

Hello. She was in a real, honest-to-God bondage dungeon. She couldn't remember ever feeling so out of her element. Not even that one time when she'd gone with Kristy to that freaky art exhibit downtown, where people wearing plastic clothes handed out free samples of condoms, and rows and rows of tables loaded with sex toys lined the enormous warehouse. That had been years ago, when they'd been in high school. Catholic high school. She hadn't even known what half those sex toys were for.

Maybe she should've known then that her friend wasn't exactly cut from the same cloth as she. But like her therapist had said, she'd probably just wanted to believe what she'd wanted to believe, rather than seeing her friend as she truly was.

It had taken both her therapist and Kristy two weeks to prepare her for this. Already, she was ready to go home. There was only one thing, or rather two, keeping her from turning on her heels and saying *sayonara* to Twilight forever. And that thing, or things, weren't the ones she'd expected.

Instead of staying to find out more about bondage, or more specifically why anyone would want to seek out a Master, she wanted to find out a little more about the godlike men Kristy was waving at.

"Hi, Master Rolf," Kristy said, reaching behind her, no doubt to catch Wynne's hand and coax her up closer.

Master Rolf. Guess he wasn't an employee. Wynne was happy to stay where she was for the moment, thankyouverymuch.

Kristy motioned to the second man. "It looks like we've both brought guests today."

Now, that raised Wynne's hopes. If the second guy—who was jaw-droppingly gorgeous—wasn't a regular at the club, then he might not be a part of the scene yet.

"Hi, Raven." Master Rolf smiled. "This isn't a guest. He's my brother, Dierk. He's taking over as general manager of the club."

Manager. That was acceptable.

"I see," Kristy responded, nodding over her shoulder at Wynne before cranking on the charm for the new manager. "It's good to meet you, Dierk. Dierk and Rolf, this is my friend Wynne. And I'm sure you can tell this is her first visit to a bondage club. She's totally new to domination and submission, so she's a little nervous."

Great. Thanks, Kristy, for pointing out I'm the new, clueless kid on the block.

She pasted on a smile, hoping they wouldn't all look at her like she was a freak. How humiliating. Maybe they'd even make her wear some kind of special badge or something.

Dierk the manager gave her a long, disconcerting once-over. Down went his gaze from her face to her toes and then slowly it meandered back up. She could almost feel his gaze as it swept over her body. Her skin felt tingly all over, her nerves twitchy and raw. "Hello, Wynne," he said in a low, rumbly voice that reminded her of a cat's purr.

The man was like sin incarnate, the very opposite of what John had been, with his sun-bleached hair and boy-next-door good looks. Dierk had dark hair, almost black, cut in shaggy, messy layers. His face was all hard angles, his eyes too dark to clearly make out the pupils. And his body . . . He was huge, built like a professional athlete, all muscles and sinew and raw power.

Kristy jabbed her in the ribs, and she realized, embarrassingly, that she'd been standing there, mute and stupid, staring like a groupie at a rock concert.

She didn't need Kristy to make her look like an ass. She was doing that well enough on her own.

Too nervous to trust her voice, she merely gave him a weak, shaky smile and nodded her head, then turned her gaze to his brother.

Master Rolf wasn't far down the gorgeous scale from his brother. There was most definitely a family resemblance. He also had that dark, wavy hair, although Rolf's was a little longer, the bottom layers skimming the tops of his shoulders. His face was as hard edged and fascinating as Dierk's, although it wasn't identical. And his body was just as big. And just as breathtaking.

Rolf offered a hand. "It's nice to meet you, Wynne. If there's anything my brother or I can do for you, just let one of us know."

"Th-thanks." Staring into his eyes, Wynne placed her trembling hand into his, expecting him to shake it. Instead, he raised it to his perfect mouth and brushed his lips over the back.

It felt like her skin was on fire, both on her hand and on her cheeks. Sure he could see the blush that had to be radiating from her face, she tugged her hand free and dropped it in front of her, flattening the other one against it.

God, she had never felt this way around a guy before, not even John. She was tongue tied, witless, practically falling over her own feet. What was wrong with her?

Nothing was wrong, she reasoned. Not a thing. It was this place that was making her all jumpy and skittery. And the knowledge of what these men probably did here.

She hadn't even dared let her gaze wander around the large room yet, although she could hear voices and the occasional snap of a leather whip.

Adrenaline pounded through her body, fueling her instinct to run, making her stomach twist and palms sweat. She swallowed hard a couple times.

". . . which is why my friend Wynne is here today. She'd like to watch, learn a little about the lifestyle, why people choose to play domination and submission games," Kristy explained. "And she's looking at it from the submissive side, which is why I'm not much help to her."

Geesh, Wynne hadn't even realized Kristy had been talking that whole time. She'd been distracted by the two gorgeous brothers. Or maybe it was the loud pounding of blood in her ears that had muffled her friend's soft voice. She could only hope that Kristy had stuck with the plan. It was simply too embarrassing to admit she was coming here to find out why her fiancé had dumped her for a gay Dom. So instead, they'd cooked up this story about her writing a romance novel about a woman's first experience with BDSM.

"I can show her around," Master Rolf volunteered, "since my brother's going to be busy all night, handling some important general manager–type things."

Something flared in Dierk's eyes. Wynne wondered what it was. But he didn't say a word.

"That would be great! I was hoping you'd offer, since I have an appointment in a few minutes." Kristy gave Wynne a gentle shove, making her feel like an unwanted little sister.

Wynne turned a scowl at her pushy friend and whispered, "Stop that."

Kristy gave her an encouraging nod. "I've known Master Rolf for years. You'll be perfectly safe." Then she hauled her huge tote over her shoulder and scampered off, leaving Wynne with the wicked-looking Master Rolf and his equally dangerous brother Dierk.

Dierk promptly excused himself to handle those "important general manager things" Rolf had mentioned.

Rolf stepped forward, crowding her personal space, and placed a hand on the small of her back.

Her muscles instantly tightened, from the waist up, and her breath hitched in her throat.

Totally ignoring her reaction to his touch, he leaned closer, murmuring, "So tell me, how much do you want to know about domination and submission?"

Nothing. Not a single thing. "Only enough to make me dangerous," she said, trying to sound at ease but failing, big time.

He grinned, the expression a fairly good interpretation of the Cheshire cat. "Hmmmm, I like that answer."

And she liked the way he'd said those words. His voice had a gritty edge to it, a sensual just-rolled-out-of-bed tone. It made her feel warm inside. Soft and feminine, too.

"Have you read anything on the Internet? Do you know anything about the lifestyle?" he asked as he steered her around a piece of furniture she couldn't name with that hand pressed to her back.

"Absolutely nothing," she said, musing at how amazing it was that a gentle exertion of pressure, shifted to the right or left, could guide her, kind of like a bridle on a horse.

"Then we'll start with the basics." He stopped in the center of the room. "This is our general bondage dungeon. In this room, our members play domination and submission games. During play, there is one general rule that must be adhered to by all participants. The activities must be safe, sane, and consensual. Safety is always the primary concern, and as you will see, we have personnel positioned throughout the building to make sure no one is hurt while on our property."

"That's good to know." Her gaze skipped past the pair of people standing next to a huge wooden cross thingy, to the big guy standing in the corner, wearing a black shirt with the word Twilight scrawled across the front.

"No one is ever forced to participate in a scene, ever," Rolf continued. "Our members are carefully screened, and no one who has had a criminal conviction is permitted access to our facilities. . . ."

She nodded, following Rolf's lead as he continued toward the back of the room. He pointed out the various pieces of furniture, naming them. He explained the general rules of bondage play. To her relief, he didn't make her stand there and watch the people who were playing. Whether it was because he sensed she was still too nervous and shaky about this whole thing or because it was a courtesy issue to the people playing, she didn't know.

"Also, there are limits to what kinds of activities are permitted in our dungeon. We have private rooms available for members to rent, and some members lease private suites, in which they can participate in more intimate activities. But out here, we don't permit any exchange of bodily fluids, including sexual intercourse. Members sanitize all equipment when they're through. In addition, our staff goes through at the end of the night and does a thorough cleaning."

This was nothing like the free-for-all kink-fest she'd imagined when her friend had tried to describe it. Quite the opposite, it seemed like the people who ran Twilight were very conscientious, responsible, and professional.

Finally, when they'd come full circle, back to the bar, he motioned to a stool. "How about something to drink?"

"Sure." She could use a stiff drink right about now. Might help her relax. "Do you have a wine list?"

"No, I'm sorry, this bar serves strictly nonalcoholic beverages. But we serve wine downstairs in the restaurant. I'd be happy to take you down there if you like."

"No, no. That's okay. I'd be just as happy with a cola. Thanks."

As he ordered her drink, she glanced at the clock, surprised to discover that her little tour had taken almost an hour. She wondered how much longer it would take Kristy, aka Mistress Raven, to finish up her appointment. Since Wynne hadn't seen her friend during her little excursion, she assumed the appointment was in a private room or suite. She tried to imagine what her friend might be doing.

Her cheeks burned.

"There you are, one cola." Rolf set the drink on the bar.

She swiveled her stool around to face the bar, and glancing sideways at her host, gave him a grateful smile. She lifted the glass, taking the straw between her lips and pulling in a mouthful. Ahh, cold. Refreshing. "Thank you for taking the time to walk me around. I'm sorry if I'm keeping you from . . . anything."

God, how lame did that sound?

"It was my pleasure." His gaze was razor sharp, piercing, as it captured hers. He held a glass in his hand but didn't lift it to his mouth. Instead, he simply sat there, staring into her eyes, watching her. His lips curled into a teasing grin. "Now that we've covered the basics, are you ready to get down to business?"

Oh God. What was he suggesting? She eased the drink from her mouth, thankful for the fact that she hadn't spewed cola all over his face.

"I . . . um . . ." If her face hadn't been roasting before, now her cheeks felt like twin electric burners, cranked up to high.

He chuckled and the sound vibrated through every cell in her body, or at least it felt that way. He plucked the straw out of his glass and set it on a napkin. "You know what they say about writing, 'write what you know.'"

"Yes, they do say that." She gulped down several mouthfuls before even trying to say another word. "I don't think I'm ready for any firsthand experiences. Today. But, thanks. I'd rather ask you a few questions, if that's okay."

"Sure, shoot away." He finally took a drink from his glass. She used those few seconds, as he tipped his head back and swallowed, to think up a few safe questions to ask. This man, this disturbingly gorgeous man, really set her nerves on edge. Whether it was the way he looked or the way he looked at her, she couldn't say. But there was something about him that made her feel funny inside.

"First, can you tell me why your members like to play these domination and submission games?"

He set his empty glass on the bar, waving to the bartender for a refill. He ordered one for her, too. "Well, I'm no psychiatrist, so I can't say why every person here gets into power play, but I can speak for myself."

She practically held her breath, waiting for his response.

"For me, it's a drive—a need—that was inborn. When I was a kid, I told myself stories as I lay in bed. Stories in which I was the mighty warrior, slaying the enemy and conquering the princess. I'd haul her away from her castle, taking her to my domain, where I was master and lord. And then I'd seduce her until she was trembling, on her back, willingly submitting to me, relinquishing everything she had, everything she was."

Wynne could picture the scene he described in her mind's eye. And much to her surprise, her heart was pounding, her body trembling, as she imagined herself in the role of the princess, stolen away to this dark and powerful lord's castle.

God, that was sexy.

No, beyond sexy. It was thrilling. Intoxicating.

"Later, I learned that there are others like me," he continued, "who felt the need to dominate. My brothers, all of them, are like me—Doms."

All. That meant Dierk, too.

Rolf continued, "Together, we gradually discovered people who needed men like us, submissives, and Twilight was born. This was a place where we could come together, without fear, without facing prejudice or judgment. It's a place where we're safe. We understand each other, we feed each other's needs, souls."

"It sounds very . . ." Powerful? Nurturing.

"Hey, there you are," Kristy said behind her.

Intrigued but also ready to call it a night, Wynne glanced over her shoulder. "Yep, here I am."

"Ready to go?"

"Uh, sure." Wynne gave Rolf one last smile. "Thank you again. It's been very . . . enlightening."

"You're welcome."

As she stood on legs that felt no sturdier than a new sapling being pummeled by gale-force winds, he caught her wrist, forcing her to turn around. "Come back and see me. Tomorrow night. We'll talk some more."

"Um . . . Maybe I could do that."

He nodded. "Yes, you could." Slowly, his smile widening, he unfurled one finger at a time, until her wrist was free. She shuffled after her friend, her gaze focused on the exit, knowing that if she didn't squeeze a full inhalation into her imploded lungs in the next few seconds, she'd pass out.

That had been the wildest rush she'd ever felt in her life. It left her feeling full of energy. Like she was buzzed.

Maybe that was the secret to this thing? Maybe the participants were looking for adrenaline? A natural high? She could admit a part of her was already demanding another dose.

This was dangerous. Passion and desire, blended with fear and anticipation. If she were smart, she'd never step foot in that place again.

3

"You owe me one thousand dollars, little brother." Dierk pointed at his computer monitor, now displaying a hazy black-and-white image of the dungeon's main exit. He'd watched the hot little brunette, with her sweet face and soft body, pass through that door no more than a handful of minutes ago.

Naturally, he wouldn't admit to Rolf that he hadn't caught her leaving by chance. The truth was, he'd watched her, unde-tected, for the past hour. He hadn't glanced away once.

It had been sixty torturous minutes, witnessing her every move. He'd seen the way her expression had slowly relaxed as his brother had brilliantly talked her through her fears, the tension leave her shoulders, her neck, her face.

Ironically, it was because of Rolf that she'd stayed longer than a half hour. Rolf could have easily scared her off. Either Rolf didn't care about the money, or he was as intrigued by the little brunette as Dierk was.

Not looking particularly put out, Rolf pulled his wallet from his pocket and peeled off ten Ben Franklins, placing them in Dierk's outstretched hand. "That was worth every penny. Damn, it's been a long time since I've played with a fresh one."

"She's something, eh?" Dierk asked, trying his damndest to keep his tone neutral as he pocketed the money. She was fresh, all right. Dewy skin and soft curves. She smelled like peaches. He bet she'd taste sweet, too. He'd spent the past hour imagining what she might taste like.

"Yeah, something," Rolf said, almost sounding star struck. He flopped into the chair opposite Dierk's and kicked his booted feet up onto the desk's polished top.

Dierk knocked them off. "Too bad she won't be back." For some reason it was really bugging him that he hadn't gotten a chance to talk to her more, to hear her lush voice as she explained why she'd come to his dungeon.

"Who says she won't? I invited her back tomorrow."

A ripple of heat sizzled through Dierk's body. He hurried to the minibar next to a file cabinet and poured himself a brandy. He downed it in one swallow. "She's not going to show up. Did you see the way she looked at everything? At you, me, our members. Like we've got two heads and are about to eat her alive. We've both seen that look before."

Setting his empty glass down, he poured one for his brother, but Rolf declined. Since it would be a damn crime to let good brandy like that go to waste, Dierk closed his eyes and tipped back the glass. The brandy slipped down his throat, warming his belly. More erotic heat charged through his system, sparked by the combination of some damn fine brandy and an even better image of Wynne flashing in his mind.

"Well, at least on that last count, she's probably right. Given the chance, I'd eat her alive," Rolf said.

The two shared a laugh.

"How about another bet? Double or nothing?" Rolf offered.

"I'm listening." Dierk filled and emptied his glass a couple more times before heading back to his desk. Tired of sitting, he leaned a hip against a bookshelf and crossed his arms over his chest.

"I'll bet our shy little writer shows up tomorrow. If I'm wrong, I pay you two thousand."

Dierk thought about it for less than a handful of seconds before handing Rolf back his money. "You're going to lose, but what the hell?"

"We'll see about that." Rolf offered his hand.

"You're on." He gave his brother's hand a quick shake then forced himself back into the chair. Frowning, he swiveled around to glance at the computer monitor. If it weren't for Rolf and the angel-faced Wynne, this job would be absolute torture. Boring beyond belief.

Whatever the problems were that Shadow had vaguely mentioned, they had nothing to do with the way the place had been run. Everything was in order, files up to date, bank accounts balanced, payables paid. Which meant he had nothing to look forward to tonight but hours of alternately staring at the security monitors and playing solitaire on the computer.

Dierk sighed. "So tell me, baby brother, why didn't you want this job? Looks like it's a no-brainer. Practically runs itself."

Rolf shrugged. "Like Shadow said, I like to play. I didn't want to work here. Are you hating it as much as I thought you would?"

"More."

"Damn. Sorry, bro." To his credit, Rolf looked genuinely apologetic.

"No reason to apologize." Dierk hit a few keys, switching the monitor to the camera focused on the St. Andrew's cross. A scene was just getting started, a Dom and his female submissive. The Dom was securing his sub's arms to the cross. "It's not your fault. No one made me take the job. I could have said no."

"No, you couldn't. For all your rebellion, we all know that you have never refused Shadow. Why is that, by the way?"

"Long story."

"Well, we've got lots of time. The club doesn't close for hours. . . . Hey, who's that?" Rolf circled around the desk, peering over Dierk's shoulder. "Ohhhh, damn."

"What's the problem?"

"Move the camera that way." Rolf pointed at the left edge of the screen.

Dierk hit the keys, remotely adjusting the camera's angle until it focused on Master Nevin, standing next to a tall blonde. Human, no doubt.

"Shit, that's Angeleque. She's not into Nevin but she's too polite to tell him to take a hike. I should go rescue her."

"You're quite the Galahad, aren't you, bro?" Dierk glanced over his shoulder.

"Hell no, I just don't like to share my subs." Rolf clapped Dierk on the back then rushed toward the door. "It's playtime. Later."

"Yeah." Once again, Dierk found himself sitting in an office he had never wanted, *watching* the action going on in the dungeon instead of being the center of it.

This was hell.

Thanks to that hot little brunette, Wynne, his blood was simmering. His cock was hard. His balls were tight.

He wanted a fuck.

He needed to fuck Wynne.

No, that was the last thing he needed: to get involved with a new submissive, a woman who was obviously going to need some stability and patience. Neither stability nor patience came to him naturally.

What the hell was he thinking?

* * *

Rolf hurried into the dungeon expecting a fight. Now, on top of the erotic heat blazing through his body, his nerves were on edge. Muscles tight. Fists clenched. Jaw locked. Adrenaline charging through his system.

Nevin, one of his least favorite Doms at Twilight, had his most favorite submissive cornered, literally. And damn if Rolf was going to let the asshole get away with it. Without hesitating, he came up behind the guy and said, "You're late."

Nevin threw him a scowl, growling. "Who the fuck are you talking to?"

"My pet." Rolf pointed at the blonde, currently looking like she was ready to go hysterical on them, any second now.

Dammit, he'd worked so hard to get her this far. He didn't need Nevin taking her three steps back.

Angeleque was a pain slut. How she loved the whip. But she didn't handle the containment side of playing at all, due to a persistent case of claustrophobia. The girl panicked if she was blindfolded. She stopped breathing when her arms were restrained. Mummify her, and she'd probably die from terror.

And of course, Nevin just loved containment play. Mummification was his special vice.

Much to Rolf's surprise, Nevin grunted and stepped aside.

Angeleque rushed past Nevin, eyes wide with fear. "I came looking for you."

His nerves still raw, Rolf grumbled, "I've told you before. You wait for me in the lobby."

She nodded.

"Now come on." He nudged her ahead, toward his private suite. He needed relief. Now. An hour spent with Wynne had left him with balls heavier than concrete. "You've made me wait long enough."

"Yes, Master. I'm sorry for being late, Master."

He followed her, mesmerized by the sway of her hips as she

walked. The girl was a runway model, and damn, did she know how to work those mile-long legs of hers. He couldn't wait until they were locked around his waist.

He unlocked the door, ushered her inside, and then relocked the door behind them. "Strip," he barked, turning toward the bag Angeleque had carried in with her. He pulled out his cat-o'-nine tails, a dildo, anal plug, lube, and rubbers. By the time he'd filled his arms with the toys, his submissive was naked and on her knees, head bowed, back arched deliciously, full breasts thrust forward.

Her nipples were tight and hard.

His gaze fixed on those pink beaded tips. "Excellent. Now present, my pet." Damn, he'd forgotten the nipple clamps. He set the supplies on a nearby table, then went back to the bag for the forgotten clamps.

Meanwhile, his pretty plaything ran through her presentation like a pro. She learned quickly, was shaping up to be a fine submissive, despite her fear of being restrained.

He punished her first, for being late, by teasing her with the thong of his whip, letting the leather strap slide over her golden skin instead of striking her with it. Within minutes, goose bumps covered her back and she trembled, murmuring, "I will not be late," over and over, until she was nearly in tears.

As a reward, he closed the nipple clamps over her tight buds, then told her to stand against the wall, her back to him. Pressing against her back and grinding his pelvis against her soft derriere, he lifted her arms up over her head and kicked her feet apart. "Be still for your reward."

"Yes, Master."

He stepped back and sent the whip sailing through the air, snapping at her flesh, striking the top of her left buttock. She sighed but didn't move. The pink stripe the lash left behind was a glorious sight. He struck her again, this time on her right ass cheek. And again. Again. Until she was panting and hot juices were dripping down her thighs.

The heavy odor of her arousal filled his nostrils, making the weight in his balls five times more agonizing. There was nothing in this world that smelled better than a woman on the verge of coming. It was a fragrance he couldn't drink in fast enough, take in deep enough.

Intoxicating.

Quickly he tore off his clothing, leaving only his leather pants. Dammit, he wanted to fuck her. His groin was aching with pounding heaviness. But he didn't fuck his submissives. Never. He would jack off. Later, after Angeleque left him.

Damn, he hoped he could wait that long.

It was Wynne's fault. He could still see her, in his mind's eye. That sweet face. Those shyly inquisitive eyes. That lush mouth, so tempting. He'd been in throbbing pain since she'd left.

But that didn't mean he'd cheat his pet out of her pleasure. No matter how agonizing it was, he'd make himself wait. It was going to fucking kill him, but that was the way it had to be. He had to stay focused on Angeleque, on her needs, on her training.

Now that she'd received a reward, it was time to test her with some restraints. Then he'd reward her once more, reinforcing her training.

His pet loved anal play. Maybe he'd fuck her ass with a dildo. Yes, that was what he'd do. That way, he could imagine he was pounding his rod into Wynne's tight little anus. He was nipping Wynne's slender neck. He was sinking his fangs into Wynne's soft shoulder. He was hearing his name murmured in Wynne's voice, as she sighed in ecstasy.

"This way." He helped Angeleque onto the bondage table, positioning her on her back, spread eagle. "It's time for your test. See if you've been doing your homework."

"Please have mercy on me," his submissive begged, her eyes filling with fear.

"I'm nothing if not merciful, my pet." Moving slowly, he fastened one cuff around Angeleque's slender ankle. He leaned over her, brushing his mouth across her lush lips in a soft, teasing kiss. "But that doesn't mean I have infinite patience. Believe me, you don't want to try me today."

4

"Wellll?" Kristy gave Wynne a sidelong look as they trotted across the parking lot. Finally, Wynne felt like she could breathe freely. Fresh air. So good. Such a relief.

Wynne knew what Kristy was hoping to hear, but that wasn't what she was going to hear. As Wynne reached Kristy's car, she admitted, "I'll give you this: it's not as dirty and gross as I'd imagined."

"Dirty? Gross?" Scowling, Kristy tossed her bag into the trunk and slammed the lid.

Wynne slid into the passenger seat and waited for Kristy to take a seat before answering. "I've always had an active imagination."

Kristy stuffed her key into the ignition, the dozen or so key rings dangling from it rattling in the tense silence. "Yeah, I knew that much, but *dirty*? Seriously?"

"Um, I was kinda imagining something along the lines of one of those nasty peepshow places on 8 Mile. You know, where men jerk off in cramped, scummy cubicles . . . and there are paper towel dispensers everywhere to . . ." She didn't finish the rest of the description. There was no need. Her friend had gotten the point.

Kristy's face went absolutely white. Then pink. Then red. "What . . . ?" She waved her hands as the car rolled to a stop at the end of the club's driveway. "Do you honestly think I'd go to a place like that? Wynne? God, I'm not an idiot." She looked both ways, then pulled the car into traffic.

"I know you're not." Wynne stared out the window, watching but not really seeing the world outside roll by. "You asked for my opinion and I gave it. I'm not trying to insult you. Quite the opposite, you can take my comment as an insult to *me*. I was ignorant. I admit it." She turned her head to check and see if Kristy's face had lost a little of that color yet.

It had.

"Okay." Looking a lot less livid, Kristy gave her a half smile. "I can accept that." After a beat, she asked, "What did you think of Rolf and his brother? Hotties, aren't they? Both of them."

She nodded. "They are. Rolf invited me to come back tomorrow. To play."

"So, do you want me to bring you back tomorrow?" Kristy turned onto a freeway service drive, steering toward the entrance ramp less than a quarter of a mile ahead. "Lucky girl! Master Rolf doesn't play with just anybody. He picks and chooses his subbies."

This time, it was Wynne's turn to blush, although her color change wasn't produced by anger but pure embarrassment. "Really?"

"Yeah. And I have to say, I haven't seen him look at anyone like that before, not even his usual subs." After a beat, she added, "You didn't answer. Do you want me to drive tomorrow?"

Wynne fingered her burning cheeks. "Oh. Uh. No, thanks."

"Okay. Can you remember how to get here, or do you need me to print up a map?"

"Um, I'll be fine." Wynne dropped her gaze to her lap, where her hands were clutched so tightly her knuckles were white.

Silence.

Kristy cleared her throat as she checked the rearview mirror before changing lanes. They were rolling up on their exit already, a good thing. "You're welcome to raid my closet if you want to wear something special."

Fighting the urge to squirm in her seat, Wynne plastered on a cheerful face. "Thanks."

Kristy maneuvered the car down the exit ramp and stopped at the red light. She gave Wynne one long look and frowned. "You're not going."

"Nope."

Kristy sighed. "Okay."

They made it within a quarter mile of their apartment complex before Kristy let her have it, which, of course, Wynne knew was coming. "I wasn't going to say anything, but you are crazy if you don't take up Rolf on his offer."

"I knew you weren't going to let this drop."

"I'm your best friend. I can't."

"You're my best friend, Kristy. Which is why I was hoping you would understand."

"I do." Kristy sighed. "You aren't comfortable. You're out of your element. You don't know what to expect, how to act, what to say or do."

"And still you question my decision?"

"Yes. Because I know you're letting an opportunity slip through your fingers."

"An opportunity to do what? Figure out why my ex-fiancé is my ex?"

"No, to search yourself, to grow, to step out of the past and into the present."

"And you think I need to let some guy tie me up to do that?"

"Yes, I do."

"Why?"

"Because that's what people need sometimes when they're stuck. They need to force themselves into a corner and see what happens."

"What self-help books have you been reading?"

"None. My opinions on the subject have been formed from years of living, and observing people."

"You talk like you're a hundred. You're twenty-three. How much could you have observed?"

"A lot more than you think." Kristy put the car in park and cut off the engine. "Honey, I care about you, and that's the only reason why I'm pushing this. Promise me you'll think about it? Just go once. Go with an open mind and see what happens. I know you'll be glad you did."

"I promise I'll think about it."

"Okay. That's a start."

"You won't nag me."

"Absolutely not."

"You won't spend the next twenty-four hours telling me how great bondage and submission is?"

"Nope. I'd rather you tell me . . . and you will, after you pay Master Rolf a visit." Kristy winked.

Sweet Jesus, there were two men. Two men having sex.

"I can't look." Wynne wrenched away from a surprised Master Rolf, twisting around to face the door.

What the hell had he been thinking? Bringing her into a private room to watch two *men* playing bondage games? Didn't he know how she'd feel about this, after what her fiancé . . . ?

Shit, he didn't. How could she forget? He thought she was writing an erotica novel about bondage.

He pulled open the door, ushering her outside before cornering her in the hallway. He planted his hands against the wall on either side of her head, caging her in. "What was that all about?"

"I—I was just caught by surprise. That's all."

"Surprise?" Rolf's intense gaze swept over her features, making her face sting with embarrassment and shame. But he didn't say another word, just stood there, so close the air around her was heavily scented with his unique aroma, a blend of tangy aftershave and man.

Her body was keenly aware of how close he was. Her nipples were tingly and tight, and deep inside her belly a warm sensation was swirling round and round.

He was so much more man than John had been, not that John had been a lightweight. But Rolf's dark, roughly hewn features were such a stark contrast to John's golden-boy good looks and innocent face.

And his body, oh my. He had muscles on top of muscles. Everything was sculpted, as if chiseled from rock. Just like his brother Dierk.

Dierk. Where was he?

She'd been disappointed when he hadn't come out to greet her in the lobby. Talk about a face. His had been the star feature in at least a couple of her dreams over the past week. In fact, those dreams were what had made her decide to come back to Twilight. She'd pretty much convinced herself it was a waste of time, searching for answers here. But that last dream—the one she simply couldn't put out of her head—that had changed her mind.

Dierk, her dark and mysterious dungeon master. She just knew he had secrets. Lots of them.

"Wynne?" Rolf cupped her chin, wrenching her out of her head and back into the real world.

Oh my God. She was standing here, nearly breathless with

lust for one man while thinking of another. What was this place doing to her?

"I'm sorry, Rolf. I shouldn't be here." *Major understatement.* "This isn't for me. It was a mistake coming tonight." *Big, huge, bigger-than-huge mistake.* She expected him to move his arms, to let her go, so she could run like a sissy.

He didn't.

He pinched his eyebrows together and pursed his lips. "What's the real reason why you came here tonight?"

Why'd he ask her that?

Her cheeks were about to combust and there wasn't a single drop of spit left in her mouth. Her tongue was as dry as the Mohave. "I'm . . . writing a book."

His eyes locked on hers, he shook his head. "I'm not buying that excuse, so how about you tell me the truth?"

"But I am . . . I did . . . I'm working on a book. It's a romance. . . ." *God, I'm such a bad liar, but I can't tell him about John. I'll look so pathetic. Ack, why do I care how pathetic I'll look in his eyes? I'm not going to do anything with this man.*

"A romance, eh?" He dipped his head lower, bending his elbows to bring the hulk of his body closer to hers. A few parts of her anatomy decided they liked it. Her gray matter wasn't saying what it thought, one way or the other.

Oh God, he was so close and he smelled so good. And his mouth, it was right there. She could let him kiss her. Yes, that would be okay.

What am I thinking?

She gulped a few shallow breaths, hoping the oxygen would help kick-start her brain. It was stalled.

"You've gotten very quiet, precious."

As impossible as she thought it might be, he leaned in closer still. His body—all six feet plus, two hundred and some-odd pounds—was practically smooshed up against hers. A whisper-thin pocket of superheated air was all that remained between them.

That, and one very big, bald-faced lie.

"Are you maybe plotting out a sex scene in that pretty head of yours? Maybe I can help." He tipped his head and brushed his mouth over hers in a whisper of a kiss.

The air somehow seeped out of her lungs, making her head spin like she was riding on a Tilt-A-Whirl. He did it again, and little currents of electricity charged through her body, starting in the center and zapping up her chest and down her legs.

Oh, this was crazy, letting this man kiss her. No, they didn't have their tongues thrust down each other's throats, but this wasn't a chaste kiss either. She was leading Rolf on, making him think things that could never be. . . .

Like she wanted him to kiss her more. Harder. Longer.

Oh God.

She turned her head and fought for the air she needed to clear her foggy head. But Rolf didn't back off. Instead, he turned his attention to her neck, sweeping her hair away to get a clean shot.

He started the torture by blowing a soft current of air against her already simmering skin. Of course, that left her shivering and covered in goose bumps. No doubt that was just what he'd hoped. Then he flicked his tongue over the pounding pulse running up the side of her neck, following it to her earlobe.

She dragged her heavy arms up and grasped the first thing that she touched, his shirt, squeezing her fingers into tight fists around the soft fabric. She heard herself breathing, felt herself melting against him, knew her resolve was melting, too, but damned if she had the self-control to tell him to stop.

It was wrong. Very wrong. But at the moment, it felt more right than any stolen kiss she'd ever experienced. Even her first with John.

He nipped her ear and her body bolted, every muscle suddenly almost painfully tight. "You're so responsive, precious. Your body reacts to everything I do."

That was no lie; even she was surprised. Not that she'd been a cold fish with John, but she'd never been so . . . easily aroused.

What a freaking understatement. God, she was on fire.

"Come with me, now. To my suite." He dropped his arms, only to take both her hands. Back-stepping, he lured her down the hall. "It's time to start your training."

5

Ohmygod, what am I doing? What. The. Hell. Am. I. Doing?
Wynne could hardly believe she was standing in a private
bondage suite. The door was closing . . . closing . . . closed.

Sure Rolf had somehow arranged for most of the oxygen to
be sucked out of the room, she gasped and backed away from
him.

He was sexy. There was no doubt about that. He had already made her feel things she had never felt before. There
could be no questioning that either. But now that she'd had a
few seconds to think, she was almost 90 percent sure this was a
giant mistake.

Surely it wasn't too late to tell him she'd changed her mind.
He wouldn't force her to stay, right?

She cleared her throat, prepared to tell him she wasn't ready
to "start her training" today, but then he sat on the couch,
kicked an ankle on top of his opposite knee, and threw his arms
over the sofa's back, and just like that he lost that scary edge
he'd possessed in ample quantity just a moment before.

"Come, sit." He patted the cushion. "Here."

Still unsure whether she was staying or leaving, she took one step forward. "I'm a little uncomfortable."

"I can tell. That's why we're going to take things nice and slow." It felt like a huge tank of fresh air had just been pumped into the room. Ahhh, she could breathe again. "We got a little intense outside. That's fine, but we need to sit down and talk first."

Yes, talk was good. Talk was safe.

Now even more relieved, she sat, leaving a fair amount of space between them. She swiveled to face him, drawing one leg up on the seat and tucking her foot under the opposite knee. "Okay." She had no idea what one would say in this situation, so she waited for him to say something.

"I need to understand what you're looking for, what your limits are, what you like and don't like."

"I'm not sure I can tell you that, since I've never done anything like this before." Was he asking about sex? Surely, he didn't expect her to tell him, a stranger, exactly what she liked and didn't like. She'd never spoken openly and frankly with a partner about sex, not even John. She'd had one hell of a time talking about it with her crazy therapist. To open up to a strange man, a Dom, would be impossible.

"But you do have some notion of your tolerance to pain."

That she could answer. "Zilch on the pain tolerance. I cry when I stub my toe."

"There, you see? You can tell me." He patted her knee and a warm current of sensual energy rippled through her. As if he sensed her reaction, he left his hand there. The longer it remained, though, the more twitchy she felt.

"Does my touching you make you uncomfortable?" he asked.

"A little."

He smiled. "I was hoping you'd tell me the truth." He moved his hand away, setting it on his own knee. "Now, tell me what you think you might gain by spending time with me in this room. And don't say you want to plot your next novel, because there are plenty of ways to learn about S and M without stepping foot in a dungeon. If there is one rule everyone must keep, without fail, it is to be open, honest. Always. You lie, you're out. Do you understand?" He gave her a pointed look that told her he wasn't about to let her get away with even a teeny-tiny white lie.

"I understand. As far as your question goes, I wish I could answer it, but I can't." Her gaze swept around the room. It was a comfortable-looking space, not quite as sterile and gymlike as the main dungeon area. Large oil paintings hung on two walls, and the walls themselves were painted a rich golden color. The couch was large and comfortable. A pretty armoire with intricately carved doors stood in one corner. With the exception of the narrow bondage table positioned against the wall opposite the armoire, she wouldn't have known it was a room that was intended for bondage play. The overall feel was sedate and sensual. Cozy, too. Intimate. Yes, that was the perfect adjective.

"If you can't tell me what you're looking for, then I'm afraid we shouldn't continue this discussion."

She turned her focus back to Rolf. A part of her could imagine him kissing her, touching her. A part of her couldn't. Strangely, she felt both drawn to him and slightly repelled. "I guess I'm expecting to learn whether this is something I want to pursue deeper or not." That was the truth, although she didn't tell him she fully expected to learn it was *not*.

"Fair enough." He gave her a satisfied nod. "Do you have any injuries or health concerns?"

"No, not that I can think of."

"Do you take any prescription or over-the-counter medicines on a regular basis?"

"Only a daily vitamin and an occasional Tylenol."

"Do you drink alcohol? Take any illegal drugs?"

"Very rarely drink and absolutely not, no illegal drugs."

"Do you see a doctor and dentist regularly? When was your last checkup?"

So many questions.

She cleared her throat and straightened up, putting both feet on the floor. "Wow, I'm feeling a little like I'm being interviewed for a job or something."

"This is a standard application. We ask every new submissive these questions."

"I see." She did, kind of. And didn't.

He explained, "It's important for me to know if you have any potential problems or limitations. My first concern is your safety and health, always. So we're going to get a feel of your overall health. What I can do, with your permission, is share the basics with the other Doms at Twilight, if you would like to approach any of them. That way you won't have to go over the same information again."

"Um, okay." The way he explained it, she could see the wisdom in asking those particular questions, as well as the many more that followed, particularly the one about being tested for STDs and HIV. She was relieved to hear all Doms at Twilight adhered strictly to the club's condom use policy, without fail. As the questioning continued, she found herself becoming more and more relaxed.

Then he asked, "Okay, now tell me how you feel about your body. Are you self-conscious about any part of it?"

That was a tricky one. She shifted nervously on the couch. "Well, don't most women have issues with some part of their body?"

"Sure, many do." He tipped his head. "What are your concerns?"

She'd never talked about her body with a man. Her girlfriends, yes. Plenty of times. Her therapist, yes. But never with a guy. Men simply didn't understand. "My butt and legs."

"Show me."

Oh god, he was asking her to strip. A little zing of jittery excitement buzzed through her body. It wasn't all unpleasant, but it wasn't exactly 100 percent good either. "I . . . okay." If she wasn't a little turned on, in addition to being utterly mortified, she wouldn't have just agreed to show her ass to a stranger. But she was a little aroused and that surprised her. Curious to see where this was heading, she decided she'd do it.

She unzipped her jeans and, keeping her gaze averted, pushed them down to her ankles. Her face was on fire by the time she kicked them off. "I inherited my mother's thighs." She pinched the soft flab on the sides and gave it a little shake so he could see what she was talking about. "My butt comes from my father." She stared at the floor.

She heard him move. A stolen glance told her he was coming toward her. Walking around her. Goose bumps erupted all over her shoulders, back, and chest.

"What's your problem with it?"

"The position of it, I guess. It's starting to move south." She cupped her ass cheeks and lifted. "I expect to wake up someday and find it has fallen to the back of my knees."

"Take off the panties."

Her pussy clenched.

He'd commanded she take off her panties. It was unexpectedly sexy, the way he'd said that.

"O-okay." She reluctantly hooked her fingers over the elastic waistband of her satin panties and pushed them down over her ass, down her legs. They moved easily from there down. She let go once they cleared her hips and they slipped to her ankles. She was too wobbly to step out of them without support, so she just stood there like that.

"Men and women look at asses in very different ways." Something touched her butt, for just a split second, and every muscle in her back, legs, and buttocks clenched. A tiny gasp slipped from her lips. "I see a soft, round, perfect ass that would pink up sweetly when it's paddled. There's nothing hotter than watching a woman's ass bouncing as she's fucked. Little hard asses don't bounce."

God, she was going to die. "I suppose not."

"Have you ever been paddled?"

Paddled? "Not since I was a child."

"Does the thought of it make you hot?"

"I'm not sure." That was the truth.

"Close your eyes." He whispered in her ear. "Imagine I'm sitting on the couch and you're bent over my knees."

That was an image all too easily conjured up. It did warm her up a little. "Okay."

"You've been bad, not terribly bad, just naughty enough to warrant a spanking. So I'll use my hand, not a paddle. The first blow stings. You flinch. Heat radiates out from where my hand strikes you. Good heat. I do it again. Again. You thank me for each one, grateful for the fact that I care enough about you to punish you. The warmth on your ass travels down between your legs to your pussy. I stroke you there and your juices coat my fingers."

Wow, she could almost feel everything he was describing. Her pussy was really warm now, her blood racing through her body, her heart thumping heavily in her chest.

"Are you wet?" he whispered, standing so close she could feel the heat radiating off his skin.

"Yes." Definitely not a lie.

"Good." He moved away and she almost stumbled, tripping over her underpants, still tangled around her ankles. "Go ahead and get dressed. I'll give you some books to read, a question-naire to fill out, and a contract. I'll let you know my decision later today. If I do accept you, I will let you know when I would like you to come back. Oh, one last question. Do you orgasm on command?"

"I've . . . never tried." She stooped down, yanked up her panties, and tripped and teetered herself back into her jeans, and then, feeling a little confused and used, she accepted the things he handed her and left.

Wow, that was one strange, nerve-racking, and intense experience. She wasn't sure whether she hoped he would accept her or not.

The next evening, after a long day at work, Wynne glanced at the Arby's and considered heading in for a quick sandwich and fries before diving into the glory of the used bookstore next door. But her raging hunger for books forced her to set aside the need for physical sustenance in favor of mental. It was late already, well past her usual dinner hour. The bookstore wouldn't be open much longer. She would rather wait another hour to eat than miss out on getting a new book. Besides, she'd rather take her meal home and settle down to eat with a good book, rather than sit in a fast food restaurant by herself and feel like a loser.

Ready to replenish her dwindled to-be-read pile, she headed into the bookstore.

Ahhhh, home. The store smelled of dust and books and incense.

After greeting the store's owner, a friendly woman of sixty-some-odd years, she made a beeline for the paranormal romance section in the back, hoping she'd find something she hadn't read already. Not far away, a man was browsing the fantasy fiction section, his back turned to her. After a quick glance around, she concluded they were the only two customers in the store.

Back to the hunt.

She just loved book shopping. It was, she guessed, her way of exorcising a subconscious drive to search and hunt and claim. Her distant relatives, a zillion years ago, might have had to search for food, hunt for prey, conquer the land. The best she could do was hunt down the perfect book, search for a new author, or perhaps wander into a new genre. By the time she left, she would be adrift in a wave of adrenaline, feeling jittery in a very good way, a hefty bag of books in her arms.

She felt herself frowning as she checked the first shelf. Nothing new. Nothing interesting. After skimming the other two shelves in the section, she turned around . . . and saw *him*.

It was Dierk, from the dungeon.

And he most obviously recognized her.

"Hello, Wynne," he said, his voice a low hum. He held a paperback novel in his hands, sort of sandwiched between them.

"Hello back, Dierk." She nodded toward the book. "Looks like you're having better luck than me today. I'm empty handed yet."

"Yeah?" He lifted the book, letting her read the cover. "It's a first edition. I've been looking for a copy for months. I never expected to find one signed by the author for less than thirty dollars."

"Really?" She reached for the book. "May I?"

"Certainly." He handed it to her. "Are you familiar with James Clemens?"

"Not at all. Is he good?"

"Excellent. I have everything he's written, both under his Clemens pseudonym and his Rollins pen name."

"Rollins?" Not really paying attention—how could she with Dierk standing there looking all amazing and talking books?—she skimmed the back cover copy. From what she did comprehend, the premise sounded pretty interesting, sort of the typical fantasy "evil versus good" theme. "That name sounds familiar."

"*Subterranean, Ice Hunt, Sandstorm, Map of Bones*—"

"Yes! *Map of Bones*. I read that book. I liked it!" She handed the book back to him.

Their fingertips grazed.

Their gazes locked.

Some kind of electricity buzzed between them, and her insides fluttered.

"It was about religious relics, right?" she asked.

"Yes." He extended his arm. "If you liked *Map of Bones*, I think you'll like this, too."

"But, it's the book you've been looking for—"

"It's okay. I'll buy it from you once you're finished, if you'll sell it to me."

"Of course I will. But I feel bad. You were so happy to have found it. What if I lose it or something?"

"Don't worry about it. My life's not over if I don't get it back. Besides, all it was going to do was sit on a shelf with the other books in the series. I'd much rather it be read than collect dust. Now, if it was a first edition, first issue of one of the first three volumes of the *Lord of the Rings*, then I might not be so generous."

"O-okay. If you aren't going to be upset." She tucked the book under her arm and touched the back of his hand with her fingertip. "Thank you." It was only a gentle graze, hardly a touch at all, but the effect on her body was absolutely mind-blowing.

A bolt of heat shot up her arm, and her face became instantly hot, like someone had smacked it. Blind reflex had her jerking her hand back before she realized what she'd done.

If he noticed her reaction, he showed no outward sign. "Maybe you can tell me what you think after you've had a chance to read it."

"I will." She tightened her hold on the book. "Although you might not want to hear my opinion if it isn't good. I tend to be pretty picky about books—"

A fingertip pressed to her lips cut off the rest of her sentence.

It wasn't *her* fingertip.

Her eyes snapped to his again, and it felt like every molecule of oxygen was sucked from the room.

He had the most amazing eyes. Dark, piercing, probing. As he stood there silent, strong, and utterly dominant, it almost felt like he was trying to invade her mind, delve into her soul. "I want to know what you think, regardless."

"Okay." Her lips brushed against his finger as she spoke, and every nerve in her skin sizzled. A tense second of silence passed between them. One magical, incredible second. Then he snatched his hand away, the abrupt way he moved making her wonder if he was feeling as overwhelmed—and giddy and nervous and happy—as she was.

He turned slightly, presenting a partial profile. He glanced at his wristwatch. "Hmmm. Gotta get back to work."

"Okay. Thanks again for the book." She waved it at him.

They exchanged smiles. Another strange, awkward, tense moment. A few seconds later, he was gone and she was dizzy. She leaned back, letting the tall, substantial bookshelf behind her support her for a few moments.

An inhalation. Exhalation. Two more. Finally, she was feeling more like herself.

Wow, that was . . . just wow.

If she'd thought her attraction to the mysterious Master Dierk had been because of the dungeon, she was mistaken. Even in the middle of a bookstore, with the most unflattering lighting known to mankind, he made her head spin.

After picking up a couple more romance novels—she was suddenly in the mood to read a hot love story—she headed for the checkout. Even after her earlier intimate exchange with his brother Rolf, the entire time she was in the store her thoughts revolved around Dierk. Every description of a novel's hero she read reminded her of him. The image of his face, those eyes, flashed through her head, over and over and over. And when she lifted her hand to her face, she caught just the slightest smell of his cologne on her fingertips. Again and again, she inhaled, drawing the tangy scent into her nose. It was masculine and spicy and intoxicating. She had to find out what it was.

"You're all set," the shop owner said, thrusting a slightly wrinkled bag at her.

Confused, she glanced down at her purse, still hanging from her shoulder, zipped shut. "Huh? I didn't pay yet."

"Your friend paid."

"Oh. He did?"

"Yes. Hang on." She signed a wide, short piece of paper and slipped it into an envelope. "Here you go. He gave me more than you needed, asked me to give you a gift certificate in the amount of the remaining money if any was left."

"Wow, how . . . thoughtful." She accepted the proffered envelope and tucked it into her purse. "Thanks."

"Thank you and enjoy your books."

Slightly off balance, she headed for her car. Once inside, she ripped open the envelope and pulled out the gift certificate.

"Oh no." It was too much.

It was too sweet. Thoughtful. Kind.

Unexpected.

She folded the ninety-dollar gift certificate and placed it in her wallet.

Somehow, she would repay his thoughtfulness.

If only she could find a first edition, first issue of the *Lord of the Rings*. And if only she had some spare cash lying around. She had a sneaking suspicion that a first edition of *Lord of the Rings* would cost a whole lot more than she had in her piddly savings account.

6

"Hey." Kristy greeted Wynne as she casually strolled into their apartment. Sitting on the couch, legs crossed at the ankle, feet resting on the coffee table, and a Snuggie wrapped around her, Kristy looked nothing like the leather-clad seductress she'd been only yesterday.

"Hey," Wynne echoed.

Kristy hadn't asked for details yet, but Wynne knew she wouldn't be able to resist for long. She wasn't going to volunteer any information if she didn't have to, partly because she wasn't sure how to vocalize her feelings. She wasn't sure what she was feeling about what happened tonight. There were good emotions and not-so-great ones twisting and churning inside, though it seemed like the good ones outnumbered the bad.

The first thing Wynne did was kick off her shoes and curl her toes into the soft, plush carpet. "What're you watching?"

"*Tough Love*. I'm in love with the matchmaker dude. He cracks me up. But I hate the chicks. They are all so clueless. If only they'd listen to him." After a beat, she added, "If he wasn't out in Hollyweird, I'd hire him to find me a match."

"What for? I thought you were in a semiserious relationship."

"Yeah, well . . ." Kristy pulled the Snuggie tighter around her shoulders, and suddenly Wynne realized she'd been totally blind the last couple of days. Kristy had probably been so focused on Wynne's personal life because her own had fallen apart. And Wynne had been too busy trying to deflect her attention to realize it.

She quickly abandoned all thoughts of a long, hot shower, and plopped onto the couch next to her hurting friend, and threw an arm over Kristy's shoulder. "Do you want to talk about it?"

"Not really."

"Okay." Wynne gave her friend's shoulder a squeeze and then, feeling like she was invading Kristy's personal space, she pulled away a little to settle a comfortable distance away, but still close enough to let Kristy know she was there for her.

In silence, they watched the rest of the program. One girl decided a perfectly nice—though a smidge boring—guy wasn't the right match for her. A second woman overreacted when her date asked why she was still single at thirty-nine, and a third pitched a hissy fit after the host told her acting slutty was going to put her in danger someday.

Finally, with the program putting an end to their distraction, they looked at each other, and Wynne knew this was it.

"How was your session with Master Rolf?" Kristy asked.

"I guess it was . . . okay."

"Okay? That's it? Do you want to tell me what happened?"

"At first, I felt so out of place I just wanted to turn around and run out of there. And making matters worse, he took me to watch two men. It was like driving a knife into my gut."

Kristy grimaced. "Oh honey, I'm sorry. But you didn't want me to tell him the truth."

"No, I didn't, so that's the price I paid for keeping the truth from him. He didn't know. But right away he caught on to my reaction and asked me what I was doing there."

Kristy's brows rose. She bent her legs, crossing them on the couch. "Did you tell him the truth?"

"No."

Kristy looked like she was about to jump out of her skin. "Then what happened?"

"Well . . ." A few images flashed through Wynne's head and her face warmed.

Kristy keyed into her reaction right away. "Wynnie?"

"He has this way of looking at me, of touching me. And, my gosh, the way he kisses . . ." She swallowed a sigh and giggled nervously, meeting Kristy's wide-eyed gaze.

"Yeah?"

"Yeah. Before I realized it, I was in his private suite."

Kristy leaned closer. "And . . . ?"

"And I'll admit, it wasn't as scary as I thought. We didn't really do much but talk, but what we did was really . . . intimate."

"I knew it!" Kristy gave her shoulder a smack. "You're a natural submissive. That's why you and Johnny didn't work out. He needs a partner who is more dominant."

It hurt hearing that name, especially in this context. But for the first time, Wynne felt like she had a little glimmer of understanding about what had happened between them. Maybe, just maybe, it wasn't something she'd done or failed to do. And maybe she wasn't not-good-enough for him like she'd let herself believe all this time.

She simply wasn't right.

More important, after today she could say for the first time that he probably wasn't right for her either.

"Are you going back?" Kristy asked, giving her a nudge, both mental and physical.

Feeling a little better, all the way around, Wynne scooped up a throw pillow and hugged it to her chest. "He left a message on my phone, accepting me and asking me to come back again tomorrow."

"And what are you going to do? Did you call him back yet?"

"I'm still thinking about it." She dropped her chin onto the pillow. "I've been thinking about it all the way home. And now here, with you, talking is helping."

Kristy dipped down, placing her face directly in front of hers. "Well?"

"I'm thinking . . . I might . . . I will."

Kristy literally bounded to her feet and pumped her arms up and down. "Yessssss!"

Wynne broke into a hearty laugh. "Sheesh, girl! Don't get too excited."

"How could I not? This is a magical moment. At least, it's made me forget about my problems for a while."

"Well, in that case, good. Go ahead, jump up and down, do a happy dance, whatever you want."

"Beats sitting around by myself eating a whole half-gallon of chocolate moose tracks ice cream."

"Yes, it is a crime eating a whole half-gallon by yourself. But with me helping you, it's totally okay." Wynne headed for the freezer, returning a minute later with the carton and not one but two spoons. She handed one spoon to Kristy, flipped the container's top open, and plunged her spoon into the center. "Let the celebrating begin."

7

Wynne pulled on the bottom of her borrowed skirt, hoping but doubting it was covering her ass. Her purse was slung over her shoulder, the completed questionnaire and contract clutched in her fist. She'd worn exactly what Master Rolf had told her to. She was beyond uncomfortable, nervous as hell, and unsure what she was supposed to do when she arrived at the dungeon.

She checked in at the front desk and was told Master Rolf had asked her to meet him in the main dungeon. She hoped he would be in clear view. The thought of wandering around in that room looking for him had her feeling a little nauseous.

For the bazillionth time, she questioned her sanity. And for the bazillionth time, she reminded herself she wasn't doing anything dangerous and if things got out of control, she had a safe word and safe gesture and she was free to use them whenever she needed.

Making an effort not to look like a nervous newbie, she headed into the dungeon, completely distracted by the thought that her butt was hanging out of her skirt. She checked it again, brushing her hand down the back to make sure it hadn't flipped up. It hadn't.

She scanned the area. There were close to a dozen people scattered around the room. No Master Rolf.

Somebody tapped her shoulder. Hoping it was Rolf, she turned around.

Nope, not Rolf.

A cute brunette who was a carbon copy of Bettie Page handed her a folded piece of paper, then hurried away before Wynne could even thank her. Curious, and assuming it was an apology for being late or a request to reschedule, Wynne moved off to one side, unfolded the paper, and read it.

> *Your master will join you after you strip off every piece of clothing you're wearing and lay prostrate in the center of the dungeon. Failure to meet your master's demands will result in the rescinding of his offer.*

There was no signature.

Strip? Naked? This was crazy. She glanced around the room. Nobody seemed to notice her practically cowering in a corner. They were all busy doing whatever they were doing: whipping, paddling, chaining, writhing. Perhaps they were accustomed to this sort of thing and would completely ignore her?

She could only hope!

She briefly considered a hasty retreat. Public nudity wasn't exactly something she was ready to explore. But then again, a small part of her was anxious to go for it, throw caution to the wind and see where this led. She couldn't deny she'd enjoyed herself yesterday.

And what if he saw her? Dierk? Her pussy warmed. What if he was watching right now? With one of those security cameras. Trying not to make it obvious, she glanced at the closest one, positioned over the dungeon's entry.

Oh hell, what did she have to lose? A little self-respect? She'd made a bigger fool of herself before and lived to tell the tale. She glanced to her right. The woman chained to the big cross wasn't a perfect size two, but it wasn't stopping her.

And that woman over there, kneeling, she had her fair share of cellulite, too.

Just go for it. You can do this.

Maybe.

It wasn't the easiest thing she'd ever done, undressing in a large room full of strangers. But, shockingly, it wasn't the most difficult either. She stood off to one side, partially hidden by a tall swing suspended from a metal frame. Nobody seemed to care what she was doing.

But she felt very small and vulnerable as she padded barefoot out to the center of the dungeon. Trembling hands clenched together, she lowered herself to her knees and then lay flat on the floor. The position, she quickly realized, was a relief. She felt somewhat hidden, since her vision was restricted.

"Well done." It was Rolf's voice. She lifted her head, but he stopped her, gently pressing it back down. "I didn't release you yet. I have asked some fellow Doms to join me in a moment, and this is the position I need you to hold."

"Okay."

"Yes, Master," he corrected.

"Yes, Master."

She heard footsteps approaching, lots of them. Her heart beat harder, faster as they came closer. She was surrounded by people. She had no idea how many. And her ass was out there for them all to see. If only the floor could open up and swallow her whole, right now.

"This is a new submissive, Wynne," Rolf said. "I would like you to tell me what you think of her ass."

One man said. "That is one of the freshest asses I have seen in a long time."

"I agree. Spankable," commented another.

"I bet it'll pink up really nice for you," suggested a third.

"May I touch it?" asked a fourth.

Instinctively, Wynne clenched her butt muscles.

"Oh nice. Look at that," commented a fifth.

"You're welcome to touch, but only the ass," Rolf told them.

Oh God, she was going to die of embarrassment.

Instantly, there were hands all over her butt, stroking, squeezing, massaging, slapping. At first, she was sure she was going to die of mortification, but gradually, after it went on for a while, the awkwardness faded and she started to enjoy the touches. It helped when she closed her eyes and imagined a certain person stroking her.

Dierk.

Was it possible he owned a pair of those hands that were kneading, pinching, smacking?

Such obedience.

Dierk focused the security camera on Wynne and zoomed in. If she truly hadn't been in a dungeon before, it was remarkable that she would go that far the first time. Rolf had discussed her application with him last night, and he knew the little brunette's main issue was a body image problem. He'd trained plenty of submissives with body image issues and none of them had stripped bare in a crowded dungeon the first time.

The girl had guts. He admired her for that.

He also admired her ass. It was round like he liked them, and he was sure it would pillow a hard cock very nicely. Too bad it wouldn't be pillowing his.

He wasn't too proud to say he wished he was out there touching her smooth skin, rewarding her for her obedience. Rolf would do a fine job training her. She wouldn't be difficult, she'd already proven that. She didn't need a harsher, more demanding master than his brother, and still he burned to be the one to bring her to the brink of her limits.

Rolf glanced up at the camera, as if he knew Dierk was there watching. Rolf narrowed his eyes for a split second then bent over and commanded Wynne to rise up on her feet.

He would take her to his private suite now. A flare of jealousy burned through Dierk's body.

The cameras in Rolf's suite had been shut off. He'd done that out of respect for his brother, a show of trust. But he was damn tempted to power them up. He could always come up with some excuse why they had to be switched on.

He reached for the computer that ran the system. His fingers hovered over the keys as he sat and watched Wynne and Rolf walk out of the main dungeon and down the single corridor that led to all the private suites. He watched them stop at Rolf's door. He watched them go through it . . . watched the door close. . . .

Should he? Shouldn't he? No, he wouldn't.

Gritting his teeth, he went back to the grunt work he'd been doing before she'd come in: ordering supplies for the bar. But he couldn't stop thinking about her. Actually, he hadn't stopped since he'd first seen her, and it was driving him nuts.

This was the last thing he needed.

Well, she was here, back in Rolf's private bondage suite. Glancing around, she could see it didn't have the same vibe it had last time. The walls were still painted the same hue. The artwork still hung in the same place. And yet, the room had taken on a more sinister feel. The table, which had been pushed against the wall, was now positioned in the center of the room. And the armoire doors hung wide open, the contents on display.

This was it. They weren't going to chitchat today.

She had no clue what she should do once they were closed

inside. Head over to the couch and sit? Climb up on that table? What?

After her gaze took a final lap around the room, she gave Rolf a questioning look.

He circled her. "Every Dom-sub relationship is different, so do not assume that what I want is what another Dom would want and vice versa."

"Okay."

"First, I will teach you how to properly kneel." He pointed to a spot not far from the entry. "Here."

She went to the place he indicated and knelt, resting her bottom on her heels.

"No, not like that." He gently positioned her with his hands, lifting her up off her heels, lowering her head, arching her back. His touches were firm but not harsh, and his nearness was both unsettling and a little arousing. "Much better." He sounded satisfied.

"Thank you. Master."

He took a step back and crossed his arms over his chest. "Now, I will teach you how to present yourself to your master."

She wondered what that involved. "Okay."

"Whenever you enter this room, you will present yourself to me. What that means is you will take your position—standing if I am standing, and kneeling as I showed you if I am sitting—and wait for me to instruct you on what to do next. When you are presenting in a standing position, you will stand like this." Once again, he used his hands to position her. Spine arched, arms held close to her sides, hands clasped behind her back, head down, shoulders back. "Yes, very nice."

Like earlier, his touches were authoritative, not exactly sensual, but still pleasant. He didn't touch any part of her that would be considered an erogenous zone, but she tingled all over anyway. His scent wafted to her nose, carried by the slight breeze his movement stirred. Heat radiated from his body, warming her as he circled around her, checking her position.

When he rounded her side, he tapped her bottom lightly. He stopped directly in front of her.

She stared down at his knees.

"You have surprised me today, precious. If you had any doubt that you're a natural submissive, you should completely dismiss it. You are obedient, gentle, and eager to please, and any master would be lucky to have you. I expect several here at Twilight will approach me, to ask if they might train you. Because we have no contract between us, binding you to an exclusive relationship with me, you are free to accept an invitation from any Dom you like."

Would Dierk be among the Doms who would approach her?

"O-okay," she responded.

Rolf clasped his hands behind his back and strolled around her again. "You need not worry about your safety. All Doms at Twilight are committed to following our guidelines. To the letter. With your permission, I will file your application in the office, so that any Dom you scene with will have access to it."

"Okay." Right now, there was only one Dom at Twilight she wished to scene with, outside of Rolf. Dierk, of course.

She felt a little guilty about the fact that they were brothers. Rolf was gentle and encouraging, polite and patient, no doubt a good master for someone who was new to BDSM. But she couldn't help feeling like she was doing something wrong because of her attraction to—correction, fascination with—his brother.

Maybe, if Dierk wasn't interested, she'd be better off choosing a Dom who wasn't his brother?

"One last thing and then we'll be finished for today." He patted the table. "Your reward."

She slid up on the table, sitting with her legs dangling over the edge.

"How often do you masturbate?" he asked.

Her cheeks burned. Would she ever get used to talking so frankly and openly about this stuff? "Uh, not very often."

"Do you have a hard time making yourself come?"

An even more awkward question. She shook her head and muttered, "Generally no."

"Good." He headed toward the armoire. "Do you use a toy or just your hands?"

When would this line of questioning end? "Usually just my hands."

"Have you tried a dong? Dildo? Vibrator?"

"I have."

He pulled out a wrapped dildo, medium sized, pretty much comparable to the average guy's penis, and pretty darn lifelike. He unwrapped it, rolled a fresh rubber onto it, then handed it to her along with a tube of lube. "Okay." He took a step back and nodded. "Go ahead."

Go ahead?! "Masturbate? Now? Here?"

"Yes, now. Would you deny yourself the reward you've earned?"

"No, but . . ." She'd never touched herself in front of anyone before. She wasn't sure if she could make herself come when she knew she was being watched. She stared down at the rubber cock in her hand for a moment and then glanced at Rolf.

He didn't look pleased. "I said, masturbate."

Oddly his demand made her heart beat a little faster, little tingles spread through her system. Maybe the apprehension and vulnerability would work to her advantage?

"Y-yes, Master."

She tended to come more easily when she was on her back, legs bent and spread wide apart. So she squirted some lube onto her fingertip, closed her eyes, lay down, and touched her clit.

Ooh, nice.

She set the dildo on the table, leaving it within reach, and used her free hand to part her labia. Oh yes, that felt good.

She started with slow circles, using gentle pressure. Gradually, things started happening. Little ripples of pleasure spread out from her center and her body started tightening. Stomach. Legs. Chest.

She increased the speed and pressure of her touches. It didn't seem to be hindering her, knowing Rolf was standing nearby watching her. Waiting. In fact, it seemed to be helping. When she imagined him focused on her pussy, a wave of heat rushed up her chest.

Then she imagined Dierk was the one watching, and her blood began to boil. She clenched her pussy around burning emptiness, and reached blindly for the dildo.

She wanted to be filled, needed to be filled.

Getting closer.

Still stroking her clit, she pushed the dildo into her pussy as far as it could go, then clenched her muscles to amplify her pleasure. In her imagination, she saw Dierk standing over her, looking on sternly, her Master, waiting impatiently for her to come.

Hot. So hot.

Her legs began trembling. She stretched them as wide as she could and worked the dildo in and out in a steady rhythm that matched the rapid strokes over her clit. Her blood was pounding through her body now. Her skin was tingling all over. Sweat was trickling from her hairline. She kept going, driven to orgasm to please him. To please her master.

His dark eyes. She saw them in her mind's eye. His lips. His hands. Tapered fingers. Thick arms and hard, muscular body.

Her master. Master Dierk.

Her pussy clenched tighter. She was going to come. So close. Right there.

"Stop," Rolf demanded.

Stop? She jerked her hands away from her quivering pussy. She'd been so fucking close. One more stroke. One more thrust and she would've been done.

Gasping and shaking and hot, she opened her eyes and looked at him. He was standing directly in front of her, with a perfect view of her burning pussy.

"Once you've caught your breath, you can start again."

"That was harsh." She started to draw her knees together, but he stopped her with a glare.

"You'll thank me later. Don't hide *my* pussy from me."

His pussy. Wowwwww. Did that stoke some flames.

She really did get into this stuff. It was sexy and exciting, a dark thrill. "Okay." She took one slow, long inhalation and released it. "I'm ready."

He nodded. "Begin."

Her pussy was still tingling and wet, and it didn't take long for her to be shaking and burning on the verge of ecstasy again. She had her imagination to thank for that, as much as that thick dong gliding in and out of her clenching pussy. The images she conjured of Dierk were almost enough to make her come without touching herself.

Hot. Hotter. Tight. Wet. Need wound through her body and pulled her muscles into knots. She gasped and arched her back. "Please let me this time."

"Let you what, precious?"

"Come. Please."

"Not yet. Hold on."

She stopped thrusting the dildo inside, just left it buried deep in her pussy. She slowed the strokes over her hard little clit, squeezed her eyelids closed and held her breath, hoping she could stop herself from coming.

"Not yet."

Ohh, this was hard. And frustrating. And ohmygod, thrilling.

She started shaking more violently, and it felt like huge waves of searing heat were billowing up her body.

Almost. One more stroke.

She stopped her hand. Her pussy twitched.

"Now." Rolf whispered, his voice sounding exactly like Dierk's. In that instant, she let it be Dierk's. She passed her finger over her clit, pulled the dildo out, and jammed it in one last time. As an inferno blazed through her body, her back arched off the table. He said over and over, "Sparrow. Sparrow. Sparrow."

Sparrow. She was a bird, flying, soaring, and swooping through the air, carried on a hot, turbulent current.

The contractions lasted and lasted. The rush pounded through her body again and again. It was an orgasm unlike any she'd ever had. Longer, and a hundred times more intense. So strong she felt it in every single cell of her body. From her scalp to the soles of her feet.

"Ahhhhhhhhhh," she heard herself say as she rode wave after wave of ecstasy.

She had finally learned what an orgasm was supposed to feel like. And now that she had, she couldn't wait to have another. And another and another.

With him. With Dierk. Even if it was only in her imagination.

Dierk gave his rigid cock one final swipe and heaved forward as his cum surged up and out, spilling into the trash can sitting at his feet.

Holy shit, what that little submissive did to him.

She was trouble, not because of who she was, but because of what she made him want.

He wanted her.

He wanted love.

But he couldn't have either.

8

Dierk wasn't so much angry when he saw his brother Rolf pull Wynne's file and hand it to Zane as he was concerned. There'd been rumors—which Zane denied, of course—that he didn't exactly respect his submissives' hard limits.

Being a Dom himself, Dierk knew there were times when a submissive might appreciate his or her limits being tested. And he also recognized the fact that there could be a fine line between testing limits and breaking them. So, he had put Zane on formal probation, warning him he would be watched at all times, including when he was in his private suite.

Zane had taken it better than Dierk had expected.

Still, Dierk had good reason to be worried when he heard that Zane was interested in scening with Wynne. She was very inexperienced and had little understanding of her own needs and limitations as a submissive yet.

"I think it's a bad idea," Dierk told Rolf when he returned to the office, Wynne's file in his hand.

"She said she was open to scening with other Doms."

Dierk leaned forward, narrowing his eyes. "And after what

you told me about Zane my first night, you feel comfortable with this?"

Rolf glanced down at the file. "Not 100 percent, but if we both keep an eye on him, he won't have a chance of getting carried away."

That was bullshit. "Why even give him the chance?"

Studying Dierk's face, Rolf set the file on his desk. "Because I felt Zane would give Wynne something I can't. She's searching yet, and I think it's unfair to vet her options for her. She's not mine. She made it clear she isn't ready to commit to me or any other Dom."

Dierk snatched up her file and opened it. He skimmed her application. "She doesn't have enough experience to know if she's over her head."

"She has her safe word."

Dierk waved Wynne's file. "Are you convinced she'll use it?"

Rolf's nod was emphatic. "Yes. Positive."

Dierk wasn't so sure and his doubt must have shown, based on his brother's reaction.

Rolf's eyebrows rose. "You told me three new submissives joined the club this month. Not one. Three. Why is it I haven't heard a word about any but Wynne? You've asked me how her training has been coming every single day." Rolf crossed his arms over his chest. "What's up? You have a thing for her? She's pretty enough, so I couldn't fault you if you did."

"No, I don't have 'a thing' for her. You know I don't get emotionally involved with submissives."

Rolf mumbled something.

"What was that?" Dierk asked.

"Um, just making a comment about the weather, is all."

"Yeah, and I'm Napoleon."

"I don't think I'm going to comment on that one." Rolf stood and gave him a pointed look. "The fact is, Wynne is an adult. She's free to make her own decisions. And she has a right to scene with whomever she likes. I'm not going to discourage her. Not when there's no reason to step in the way. Now, if that bastard steps outta line, I'll be the first to move in. But not before." Rolf headed toward the door. "Since you don't get emotional about submissives, I don't see any reason for you to stop her either." He yanked open the office door, forcing Dierk to bite back an expletive.

He would not let his staff see him lose control.

He counted to five, took several deep breaths, and then, after the door was shut, kicked his desk a couple of times.

There was no getting around it: he'd have to watch her scene with that sonofabitch, Zane. Warranted or not, he didn't trust him, not with any new submissive, and particularly not with Wynne. She was so delicate, fragile.

To see her spirit broken . . . he couldn't think of it.

Standing in Twilight's lobby, a black duffle bag at his feet, Rolf greeted Wynne with a smile. "There's another Dom who would like to scene with you today. Would you be interested?"

Rolf's words made Wynne's heart hop in her chest. Could the other Dom be his brother Dierk? "Can you tell me who it is?"

Rolf considered her question for a moment before responding. "I would rather take you to him and let him introduce himself."

That wasn't the response she was hoping for. "Does he understand I'm new?"

"Yes. He is *most definitely* aware of that fact."

Hmmm, the way Rolf had worded the answer to her first question had suggested it was a Dom she hadn't met before. But the emphasis he placed on the second response made her think it could be Dierk. It was too soon to break into a happy dance, but she couldn't help getting a little giddy. "Um, I'll meet him and see where it goes from there." She tried to hide her excitement, feeling it was a bit of an insult if she acted too excited. Like Rolf wasn't good enough for her.

He was plenty good enough. That wasn't the issue. She simply couldn't explain her attraction to Dierk. It was different, unlike anything she'd ever felt before. Magical.

"If you're feeling guilty, or afraid you'll hurt my feelings, you won't." Rolf lifted the duffle. "I want to encourage you to experiment, try new Doms. You may find another Dom's style fits you better than mine."

Her respect for Rolf couldn't be greater. "That's very understanding."

He handed her the bag. "I hope you'll accept this."

"What is it?" Unsure how to respond, she took it from him.

"I know you don't own any gear yet, so I bought you the basics to get you started."

"Wow, that is so generous." That deserved a hug, which she was happy to deliver. "Thank you, Rolf."

He gave her shoulders a pat and released her. "Now that that's settled, I'll take you to the other Dom." Rolf led her through the main dungeon to the back hall, where all the private suites were located. He stopped in front of a door that was only a short distance from his and knocked.

The door opened.

It wasn't Dierk.

She tried to hide her disappointment.

"Master Zane, this is Wynne." Rolf took Wynne's hand and set it on Zane's, then stepped back. "Good-bye, Wynne."

"G-good-bye." Now really nervous, she gave Master Zane a quick up and down glance. He was big, dressed all in black. Very masculine and intimidating. Very . . . Dom.

Master Zane released her hand, took her duffle from her, and turned and walked into his private suite, leaving her to follow. Like she'd been taught by Master Rolf, she stood in the center of the room, doing her best to hold the position he'd taught her to present. Head down, arms pressed to her sides, hands clasped. Chest out, spine arched.

He unzipped her bag and inspected the contents. "I've read your profile, and I see you've had no pain tolerance training, sensory deprivation, or restraint."

"No, Master, I haven't. I wasn't really looking for any intense pain play."

"Pain tolerance training is generally part of a submissive's instruction."

Warning bells went off. "Um, I agreed to come and meet you, but I don't think this is the right situation. . . ." She started toward the door, but Master Zane stepped in front of her and gave her a menacing look.

He wasn't going to let her leave?

About to freak out, she shuffled backward until her rear end hit something.

Rolf had assured her that all the Doms at Twilight followed the rules. He wouldn't lie to her. He wouldn't trick her. No way. Granted, she hadn't known Rolf very long, but she felt he possessed a very strong sense of honor and morals.

"You must trust me." Zane circled her slowly, his gaze sweeping up and down her body.

Easy for him to say.

"I approve of your clothing. Master Rolf has been training you well." When he stopped directly in front of her, he crossed his arms over his chest. "I'm not accustomed to selling myself to a submissive, but I will tell you this: I have a great deal of experience and I am fully capable of reading a submissive's body language. I will know, before you speak a word, whether or not I've pushed you too far."

She wanted to believe him. She kind of did, but not because he inspired her trust by any word or deed. He sounded, looked, and acted tough. Inflexible. Rather, it was because Rolf had arranged for her to scene with him and she felt she could trust Rolf.

Rolf knew she was inexperienced.

Rolf knew she was unsure.

Rolf knew she had absolutely no tolerance to pain.

He had to know something she didn't, or he wouldn't have encouraged her to scene with this Dom.

She took a few deep breaths. "Okay."

"If you need me to stop completely, for any reason, you will use the word 'red.' If you would like me to slow down or ease up, you will use the word 'yellow,' and if you would like me to increase the intensity, you will use the word 'green.'"

"Yes, Master. Red. Yellow. Green."

He gave her a curt nod. "Very well. Kneel."

She knelt.

He went to the metal cabinet in the room's corner, which she assumed served the same purpose as Rolf's armoire. Sure enough, when he opened the doors she saw all kinds of ropes, chains, whips, floggers, crops, paddles, and who knew what else. It was one well-stocked bondage closet.

"I will use pieces from your kit today. You're lacking some things, but that's to be expected." He pulled on surgical gloves.

Ack. He was going to wear latex gloves? What the heck was he going to do to her?

Her heart halted then kick-started into a wild beat. All kinds of terrifying images flashed through her mind, making her wish she didn't have such a vivid imagination.

He pulled a black mask out of her bag, walked around her, and placed it over her eyes.

The world went dark.

Hands clenched tightly, fingernails digging into her palms, she kept reminding herself that Rolf wouldn't put her in danger. And there were the cameras, thank God. Somebody would be watching.

Somebody.

Dierk?

"Undress, but leave on the corset and a G-string."

"Yes, Master."

It wasn't exactly easy breezy getting herself out of the borrowed übertight latex miniskirt while blindfolded, but she managed, and within moments she was back on her knees again.

Her heart rate still hadn't slowed. If anything, it was galloping at a quicker pace.

"My focus as a Dom is not on the sexual gratification of my submissives, so do not expect any kind of penetration, not by any part of my body or even a toy."

"Yes, Master." That was actually a relief. She found she could breathe a little easier, though she did wonder, then, what his focus was. She would soon find out, that was for sure. But in the interim, she was left to wait, wonder, imagine all sorts of shocking possibilities.

This was where she was having the biggest problem in all this. So much of the excitement of BDSM was built up by waiting, anticipating. But she'd never been fond of facing the unknown. She tended to drive the same route to places, even if a shorter one was discovered. Tended to shop at the same stores. Tended to live by her routine.

Waiting, anticipating, wondering. Those weren't activities she willingly embraced.

Which was why she had surprised herself by not only enjoying her first encounter with Rolf as much as she had, but also agreeing to scene with another Dom, whose identity had been kept from her.

Her temporary master helped her to her feet and steered her toward a piece of furniture, a kneeler of some kind. He helped her get herself positioned on it: bent over a raised support, her butt up, legs wide apart. A minute later, her wrists were shackled to the supports, down near the floor.

Talk about feeling completely out of control, utterly vulnerable.

It was pretty frightening. Her spine was tight, her heart pounding with anticipation. But her pussy was also clenching as erotic heat gathered between her legs. She'd never guessed she would react this way to being tied up by a stranger. Never in a million years.

And here she'd thought she knew herself so well.

Something touched her butt. A soft something.

Totally driven by instinct, she tightened up her muscles and tucked her rear end down.

"No." His voice was harsh. The little sting of pain that followed his reprimand wasn't exactly friendly either. It took her completely by surprise, making her jerk up, yanking against her restraints.

Assuming he'd struck her—with what, she had no clue, but it hadn't hurt bad, more caught her off guard—because she'd tipped her hips down, she rocked them back, lifting her butt up again.

The touch returned, and this time, she focused on holding her position. She did okay, it seemed, that time, but then she lost it when he touched a spot that was very ticklish.

She jerked.

A deep, "No," followed, along with another whack on her buttocks.

The sting quickly turned to heat. And that heat radiated through her body in soft, slow, undulating waves. It was the most bizarre and unexpected sensation.

This time when he touched her ticklish spot again, she didn't try so hard to keep still, and, as she expected, she was punished. Once again, the punishment was more pleasurable than painful.

She was starting to feel a little giddy.

She heard Master Zane walk away, listened to the clank of

metal. She counted every single heavy footstep as he returned to her.

Another touch. This one right at the small of her back. One of her worst tickle spots. She bit her lip. There was no way she could avoid tightening her spine. Her hips rocked back, lifting her butt up higher.

There was a grunt of satisfaction. "That's not what I was expecting, either, but I like it."

Another sting. This one hurt a tiny bit, but the pain quickly turned to warmth. And that heat spread through her body again. Her breath quickened. Her heart hammered against her breastbone. A moan slipped from between her lips.

A hard slap came next, and it did hurt, and she yelped. It wasn't so bad that she would have cried or anything, but it did get her attention. That sensation she would rather avoid in the future.

But then a moment later a strange rush zoomed through her body, wild and shocking. It almost felt like she'd swallowed a pill of some kind. She felt energetic and strong and buzzed, like she'd downed a half-dozen shots of tequilla.

"Ohhhh," she heard herself moan.

Master Zane struck her again, with whatever fiendish toy he held. And again. Over and over. And each impact produced a tad more pain, but with it came a bigger and bigger rush, until she was chanting, "Green, greengreengreen!"

The sensations blurred, and she felt herself sinking, as if her soul was detaching from her mind and floating through her body. Now she could appreciate why people sought out pain. Now she had discovered a part of herself she might never have uncovered, if it wasn't for Master Zane and his wicked whip.

When he stopped, he coaxed her back to the outside world with a soft voice. She felt as if she'd traveled into the deepest parts of herself. As she made her way to the surface, she was only vaguely aware of him unfastening her wrists and easing her into his arms.

They were strong arms, steel sheathed in velvet. Capable. Protective.

She sagged against him. Her butt was still hot, but she didn't care. She cried and laughed, for reasons she couldn't really sort out. He held her until she quieted.

"It wasn't what I thought it would be," she admitted.

"You are remarkable, Wynne."

"Thank you." She smiled.

"No, thank you, for turning over your trust and allowing me to bring you to a new place."

Still giddy from the intense experience she'd just gone through, she giggled. "That you did." She gazed up, looked deep into his eyes. "Will you let me do it again sometime?"

"Whenever you wish." He showed her the whip he'd used on her. It looked pretty darn scary, with the wood handle, braided wrist strap, and narrow, knotted tails. She put it into her bag, along with the restraints and blindfold, thanked him again, and left.

She had found peace.

Her mind was still.

Her body was still.

Her soul was still.

It was heaven.

9

Wynne thought about the dungeon all week. She had dreams of Doms, shirtless, their heavily muscled shoulders and chests oiled, thickly corded limbs flexing, muscles bulging, as they climbed over her on hands and knees. It was like watching Playgirl movies all night long. She awoke feeling pleasantly tense, her pussy thrumming, her blood simmering.

She was changing; she felt it. Like a caterpillar closed in its protective cocoon. Instead of literal body parts shedding, changing, old beliefs and fears were being replaced by new ones.

She couldn't wait to go back to Twilight, to see Rolf, Zane, and, more than anyone else, Dierk. She could talk of nothing else with Kristy. She asked lots of questions and listened, sitting on the proverbial edge of her seat, absorbing every word her friend told her. Kristy talked about her kit, how to care for each item properly. She told her about the basic rules of bondage and submission, sadomasochism, as well as a little of the history of the BDSM culture. The difference between a 24/7 Master-slave relationship and casual BDSM playing. By the time Friday night had arrived, she comprehended a lot more about the world she had wandered into. And she also had a better understanding of herself and what she was looking for at Twilight.

This wasn't about understanding John anymore; it was about understanding *Wynne*. She still had a lot of insight to gain.

Once again, she groomed herself from the soles of her feet to the top of her head, and she borrowed a sexy fetish outfit from Kristy. This week, she went with a short black latex skirt and black corset. The borrowed matching shoes had five-inch heels and were überchallenging to walk in.

Unlike last time, she didn't bother with underwear.

Her heart pounded as she drove to the dungeon. Her nerves pricked. Her hands trembled.

What would happen tonight?

She was scheduled to have a session with Rolf—assuming no other Doms had requested a session with her. Would he bring her to a bone-melting climax again? How many times and how? Or would he tie her up and paddle her with her new whip? Those little strips of knotted goatskin did wonderful things to her. The tails' nips were like sexy little love bites.

She'd never experienced anything like that before.

Of course, her thoughts also turned to Dierk. She hadn't seen him in a while and still her feelings about him hadn't faded. She was just as fascinated with him as she'd been the very first time she'd seen him, even though she was 95 percent positive he didn't feel the same thing for her. She'd been there before—on the painful side of a one-sided crush—so that was nothing new.

By the time she pulled into the parking lot outside of Twilight, she was edgy and excited, nervous and hopeful all at the same time. One big bundle of tight nerves and tense muscle, wrapped in black latex.

She clacked into the building, teetering dangerously on those ridiculous high heels, and signed in at the front desk. The receptionist told her Rolf would meet her out in the lobby, so she did her best to pull the diminutive skirt down over her butt, took a seat in one of the nearby chairs, and waited.

"Wynne."

That sounded like Rolf, but it didn't. She turned to glance over her shoulder.

Dierk.

Her insides did a little happy dance. She beamed at him.

He frowned.

The happy dance came to an abrupt halt.

"What are you doing out here?" he asked, looking puzzled.

"I was told to wait here for Rolf."

He nodded, crossed his arms over his chest. Those were really nice arms.

She wished she could thank him for wearing short sleeves. It was mighty kind of him.

"Hmmm," he said.

"Is something wrong?"

"No." He stepped back. "I thought Rolf said he wouldn't be coming to the club tonight. I must have misunderstood."

"Oh." She stared at his lips then checked out the rest of his features. Gorgeous. Perfect. Really fine.

Was there nothing on the man that wasn't perfectly amazing?

"I'll give him a call." He moved toward the door she assumed led to his office. "Be back in a minute."

"Sure. Thank you."

Perched on the edge of the seat, she clenched her hands in her lap. Wasn't this just her luck? She'd been so excited about tonight, and things were falling apart.

She dug into her purse for her cell. If Rolf wasn't going to make it, was there any rule against her approaching a Dom and asking him if he would train her?

A Dom like . . . Dierk?

She decided to call Kristy now, so that she'd be prepared when Dierk returned. Just in case.

A subby had to take advantage of an opportunity as it arose. Right?

She scrolled down to Kristy's name and hit the call button. To her relief, Kristy answered on the second ring.

"Hey, girl," Kristy said. "What's up? Didn't you go to Twilight tonight?"

"I'm here now." Wynne walked over to the lobby's corner, farthest from Dierk's door, and turned to face the wall, hoping nobody would overhear her conversation.

"And you're on the phone with me?" Kristy's voice clearly communicated her confusion.

"Yeah, there might be a problem, so I wanted to ask you about protocol."

"Okay."

"Specifically, I wanted to know how a submissive approaches a Dom, to ask if he would be willing to have a session with her?"

"Hmmm. Okay. My suggestion would be to present yourself, as you would for Rolf, and wait for the Dom to take the lead. If he doesn't, then the meaning is clear."

"Okay. Got it."

"Good luck, sweetie."

"Thanks." No sooner did she end the call than Dierk was back.

Her heart kicked into overdrive, thumping along at a pace that would make a hummingbird's look sluggish. She took her position, gaze lowered, arms pressed to her sides, hands clasped behind her back.

"I'm sorry, but there was a misunderstanding," Dierk told her.

She said nothing. Instead, she remained perfectly still, silent.

He didn't speak. Didn't move. For ten seconds. Thirty. A full minute.

This was agony.

Was she doing this right? Would he understand her message? And if so, would he accept her invitation or reject it?

A heavy silence fell over her. Staring hard at the floor, she didn't hear Dierk leave the room, but because she couldn't see him, not even his feet, she couldn't be sure he was still there either.

Still nothing.

Oh God, tell me I haven't made an idiot of myself.

The softest stream of air brushed across her shoulder and her nape prickled. Goose bumps erupted over her arms.

Another gust tickled her neck. More goose bumps covered her chest.

She shuddered.

"This way," he said, his voice husky.

He said yes! Yesyesyes! She just barely managed to swallow down the wha-hooo of glee that shot up her throat.

Keeping her gaze lowered and her arms snug against her sides, she followed Dierk down the hall, through a couple of doors and finally down a familiar corridor. They went to the very last room. He stepped inside first, and she followed, taking her place in the center of the room. She set her kit at her feet.

This was it, the moment she'd been waiting for since the first time she'd seen Dierk. She was so excited, she could hardly keep still.

It wasn't easy to keep from grinning like a total dork either.

He made her wait a long, long time before he said a word. It was pure torture. Keeping her gaze lowered, her head still, she glanced around the room. His private suite was larger than Rolf's. What it lacked in design, it made up for in function. Every inch seemed to have been well planned, the bondage furniture placed to make optimum use of the space.

"You must understand we can do this only once. I don't take

members as submissives. It isn't in the club's best interest. Nor is it in mine," he said.

She wondered, if he didn't take club members as submissives, why did he need such a large, well-stocked bondage suite at the club? "I understand, Master."

"You will have no expectations outside of this one session?"

"No, Master. I promise."

"Very well, then." He left the room, exiting through a different door than the one they'd entered through. When he returned, his face was hidden by a mask. She was slightly disappointed, but of course she kept her discontent to herself.

His face was something to behold. She would have liked to study it for the next hour.

Perhaps that was exactly why he'd hidden it?

"Come here," he commanded.

She walked to him, struggling to keep her gaze lowered. Her hands were literally trembling. She was shaking all over, actually, and not because she was scared like she had been with Master Zane, and not because she was feeling unsure like she had been with Rolf, but because she had been waiting for this chance for so long. She wanted it to be absolutely perfect.

"Undress."

She started with the corset first. Looking down at his feet, but not really seeing anything, she unfastened each hook. In her mind's eye, she imagined him watching her, his dark eyes stormy, filled with raw male hunger. Once she had it off, she let it slip from her fingertips, letting it fall to the floor.

He said nothing, so she moved on to the skirt. It took just as much effort to work her way out of it as it did to get her in it. Adding an extra level of danger to the task, she was teetering on heels. She wasn't big on wearing high-heeled shoes on a daily basis, not even a moderate two inches, so she wasn't very steady on her feet. Twice he caught her at the waist and helped steady her. Twice she said a little prayer of thanks. Not because he'd saved her from injury but because of the sheer pleasure of receiving his touch.

But as soon as she had righted herself, he removed his hands. It scared her how much she longed for them to return to her.

Now she understood.

This was what drove a submissive to such ends to pleasure her Master. She got it. Yes. She understood at last. The excruciating longing and overwhelming wish to please were enough to make her do almost anything. The reward: the ecstasy of a touch.

She stood nude before him now. She didn't know whether he was looking at her or not, but she felt something, like a current of electrically charged air drifting over her skin. Down her back, around the side, and up from the floor, up her thighs, to her stomach, chest, head.

She couldn't help it, she looked at him. Their gazes locked. She stopped breathing. The world fell away, and nothing existed but the dark spirits she saw swirling in his eyes. What was it she saw? What ghosts haunted his soul?

How she wished she could learn more about this man, find out why he was possessed by such darkness.

"Do not look at me," he warned.

It wasn't easy, but she tore her gaze away. "I'm sorry, Master."

He snatched her kit up, plunked it on a nearby table and unzipped it. What toy would he choose, and what would he do with it? Anxious to get started, she listened to him searching through the contents.

"I didn't wish to start our session with a punishment, but you've forced me to."

"Yes, Master."

"The wall."

She lifted her gaze enough to see where he was directing her to go. Bolted to one wall were four chains. At the end of each chain were leather straps.

Oh yes! He was going to chain her up. Her pussy thrumming, she went to the wall and turned to face him.

He stopped her with a firm, "No."

Slightly disappointed, but not surprised, she turned around, spread her legs a little, and extended her arms out to the sides. He fastened a cuff around each of her limbs and then, without giving her a bit of warning, struck her with a whip.

The pain shot down her spine like an electrical charge, but unlike the first time she'd been whipped, she held almost perfectly still. Then the heat followed, a stinging burn, on her right shoulder blade. The second time, he struck her on the opposite shoulder blade. She curled her fingers into tight fists and braced herself for a third blow, but it didn't come.

Seconds ticked by.

She felt the endorphins charging through her body, sweeping away the pain and replacing it with a deep, urgent carnal hunger.

Would he touch her? Please? She ached for him so badly, she wanted to cry.

Still, he did nothing. He didn't release her. He didn't touch her. He didn't speak.

Her need started to ease. Her muscles gradually softened. Her lungs slowly re-inflated. She inhaled deeply then exhaled.

She heard him mutter something under his breath but couldn't make out what he was saying. Was he still angry with her? Had she done something wrong?

In any other situation, she would have turned around and simply asked him. But she couldn't. Not in this context. It was frustrating enough to make her grit her teeth.

Right now, she would pay any price to read his mind. What would happen next?

*　*　*

He couldn't do this.

Dierk unfurled his fingers, letting the flogger drop to the floor.

What the hell was wrong with him? Why did he feel the pain when those tails struck that smooth ivory skin? And why did his heart ache when he looked into Wynne's eyes?

Never had he reacted this way to a woman. He had no idea what to say, what to do. He felt like he wasn't himself any longer and that his mind, heart, and spirit had been stolen away and replaced by someone else's. Everything he'd known about himself was suddenly a lie.

What the hell?

He'd known it was going to be tough, even before he'd brought her back to his suite. But he hadn't guessed how difficult it would be to remain detached, remote, or how strong the compulsion to take her as his own would be. Not until he'd closed the door.

Now, it was too late.

He was on the verge of losing a battle. If he touched her again, if even a single fingertip came into contact with her body anywhere, he would lose the fight. He would haul her against him and wrap his arms around her little body, press her sweet cheek against his chest, and bury his nose in her hair. He would whisper sweet words in her ear, promises.

He couldn't.

He needed to stop this. Now. It wasn't fair to Wynne. He knew what he'd seen in her eyes: hope, affection, longing. She could never be his, nor could he be hers. He belonged to another. It was a matter of duty and honor.

His teeth gritted, he jerked the mask off. It hadn't done any good; he couldn't hide the truth from Wynne, no more than he could hide it from himself. He wasn't just attracted to her, he was mesmerized.

"We can't do this again." He watched her spine stiffen.

She didn't speak.

His heart heavy, he released her from the shackles. He tried not to look at her luscious body, not admire the curve of her hips, the soft swell of her stomach and the full heaviness of her breasts. Beautiful. Perfect. Temptation like he'd never seen before.

He was in hell.

He stepped back. "Get dressed and you are free to go."

"Yes, Master."

He stared down at the flogger, lying on the floor. The hurt and disappointment he heard in her voice made him want to strike himself with it.

He'd done his best, but he was too fucking weak. He couldn't stand that close to this woman and not want to touch her. He couldn't see her nude and not burn to take her. He couldn't look into her eyes and not ache to protect her.

He hadn't thought it was possible, but he had met his Achilles' heel: the one thing, or rather one person, who could destroy him.

For the sake of all of them, especially Wynne, he had to make sure he was never in the same room with her again.

"Thank you, Master," she mumbled.

Dammit. He felt his whole body stiffen. He couldn't look at her. Could. Not. Look. "Remember, we can't do this again." He headed toward the door, opened it, stepped out. But before he moved out of her sight, he turned and snapped, "And stay away from Zane."

Cursing himself, he hurried toward the club's back emergency exit. He needed some air, space, time, quiet.

10

W ell, that wasn't what she'd expected, not that she could really say what she'd been hoping for when he had finally agreed to have a session with her.

It was . . . uncomfortable, awkward, almost like he didn't know what to do with her.

Was that her fault?

Hoping she'd get a chance to talk to Kristy about it later, she slung her bag over her shoulder and left his suite, closing the door behind her. She saw a sign for a fire exit, and, feeling a little out of sorts, decided she'd go out that way, rather than tromping through the main dungeon toward the building's front.

Not sure if she'd set off an alarm, she pushed on the door. No bells. No blinking lights. She was good. She hurried out, stepping into a still, moonless night. The fresh air felt good. It brushed across her skin in a gentle current, cooling it. She took a quick look around, decided she was alone, but not exactly in the safest place. An alley, connecting the two main roads running north and south on either side of the block, ran behind the building. It was deserted, dark, and isolated.

A little tense, and shivering at the creepy somebody-is-watching-me feeling buzzing through her, she hurried toward the side of the building. As she stepped around the corner, she caught sight of a vehicle parked by the side of the building.

A few seconds later, she realized it wasn't parked.

Too late.

She screamed and tried to move, but it felt like her brain had become disconnected from her body. She couldn't react fast enough.

Something struck her from behind. The world became a blur of black and white and suddenly she felt like she was floating.

A split second later, she realized she was being carried.

Who?

Dierk. Watching the speeding car careen around the corner, she looped her arm around his neck.

Dierk had saved her life.

He stopped at the front corner of the building. They were hidden, cloaked in a heavy, cool shadow created by the lights illuminating the building's front entrance. He gazed into her eyes for a moment, then gently set her on her feet.

Unsteady and breathless, she turned to face him and swung her other arm up. She tangled her fingers in his hair. "T-thank you."

He tipped his head, bringing it closer, closer. Was he going to kiss her? *Yes, yes, yes!* She held her breath and closed her eyes.

"You're welcome." His whispered words hummed through her body like a low-voltage current.

Tingly, she rose up on tiptoes and simultaneously pulled on his neck.

"Dierk?" What was he waiting for, a formal invitation? If he couldn't read this girl's body language, he was blind.

One second passed, two, three, four, five. When her calf muscles started twitching, she sank down onto her heels. She let go of his neck, letting her arms fall to the sides.

Dierk stepped back.

She wished she could just die right now.

Suddenly, she realized she was barefoot. Where were her shoes? Her bag? "I-I think I dropped my things."

"I'll get them. Wait here." He turned away.

Still a little shaky, she watched him fade into the blackness.

She took the time while he was away, gathering her possessions, to collect her wits. Maybe Dierk was sending somewhat mixed signals. At times, he seemed to be attracted to her. Others, he seemed to be intentionally pushing her away. But most of the time, he was pushing her away.

So why did she keep hanging onto those other moments, when the chemistry between them was more potent than nuclear fission? Why couldn't she accept he didn't want any kind of relationship with her?

Was he married? Or in a committed relationship? God, that possibility hadn't crossed her mind, not once.

She wasn't sure what made her feel worse: practically throwing herself at a man who didn't want her, or imagining Dierk hugging, kissing, holding another woman.

Her mood sinking, she leaned back, letting the building support her. Dierk materialized out of the gloom a few moments later. He held some things cradled in his arms, strong limbs that had once been cradling her.

Was it possible to be jealous of a duffle bag?

"I'm afraid some of your things were damaged," he said.

"That's okay."

"I'm not sure I found everything. It was scattered. I could only locate one shoe."

"No biggie," she lied. Kristy was going to be none too happy to learn one of her expensive shoes had gone missing. But right now, Wynne couldn't care less. "As long as I have my keys and my driver's license, I'm good."

"Those, I found." He tipped his head toward the parking lot. "I'll take these to your car. Where are you parked?"

"Not far." Barefoot, she padded between some parked cars, heading for hers. She was painfully aware of Dierk: when she led him to her vehicle, when she unlocked the door, and when she bent down to flip the driver's seat forward so he could put her stuff on the back seat.

He straightened up. "Okay. Drive safely."

"Will do." Another awkward moment. "Thank you for the book store gift certificate. And thank you again for saving my life. I didn't realize that car was moving until it was too late. And then I was frozen." She chuckled nervously. "I have a new appreciation for how a deer feels when it's caught on a freeway, staring at an oncoming semi truck."

"I happened to be there." After a beat, he added, "Please don't use that back door again. The alley isn't safe."

"You have my word." She bit her lip. A part of her wanted to say something about the session, and what had happened just now, when she'd practically begged him to kiss her. The other part—the logical one—was telling her there was no point. When he turned to walk away, the illogical part took action. "Wait," she called.

He glanced over his shoulder.

"About tonight. Our session—"

"I apologize. I shouldn't have taken you back to my suite. I wasn't comfortable with it, and I shouldn't have done it."

She wrapped her arms around herself. "Did I do something wrong?"

His expression softened for a fraction of a second but then, just when she was starting to appreciate it, it hardened again. "No, you didn't do anything wrong. Like I said, I don't play with club members. I feel it's better for the club and for both of us."

"Okay." His reasoning was a little vague but still understandable, she supposed. She tried to equate it to a bar owner drinking with his customers during business hours. Bad business. "I understand. I'm sorry I put you in an awkward situation, both in the club and . . ." She couldn't finish the sentence. She felt like such an idiot.

He shook his head. "No harm, no foul." He stepped around her open door, tipping his head. "Good night, Wynne."

"Good night." She sank into the driver's seat, slid the key into the ignition, and, as Dierk closed her door, cranked it to start the engine. She watched him walk back into the club before she pulled out of the parking lot.

"How'd your session go? Wanna talk about it?" Kristy asked before Wynne was in the door. "Holy shit!" Kristy's jaw just about hit the floor once she saw Wynne, and Wynne realized, belatedly, that she must look more roughed up than she thought. "What the hell happened to you?"

"I almost got hit by a car."

"Ohmygod!" Kristy rushed to her, yanked the pile of things out of her arms, and dropped them onto the floor, then grabbed her hands and dragged her into the living room. "Are you hurt anywhere? Should I take you to the hospital?"

"No, I'm fine. Just shaken."

"Okay." Kristy visibly exhaled. "Shit, talk about giving a girl a scare. Why didn't you call me?"

"Couldn't get a signal on the cell phone." Wynne pointed at the heap of mostly torn and broken things Dierk had recovered for her.

Kristy bent down, scowled and scooped up what remained of Wynne's phone. "Um, I guess that should come as no surprise." Kristy threw her arms around Wynne and squeezed her. "Ohmygod, you weren't kidding! I'm so, so glad you weren't hurt!"

"Does that mean you won't be mad if one of your shoes is missing?"

She felt Kristy stiffen for a split second then soften again. "No, I won't be mad. You had an accident."

"I'll replace them."

"No, you won't." Kristy hurried to the couch and sat. "Come here, I TiVo'd this week's episode of *Tough Love*."

"I don't know if I'm in the mood to watch television right now." Wynne stooped next to the pile and started digging through it. Almost everything that had been in her duffle was either completely unusable or damaged. A few items were salvageable, like the leather flogger.

More than ever, she realized how close she'd come to losing her life. It was truly a miracle she wasn't dead.

She went to the kitchen and got the trash can and, after changing into some pajamas, started sorting through her things, dumping the junk in the can.

Kristy came over, sat beside her, and started helping her. "Outside of the disaster, how did your session go? You called me, so I'm curious to hear what happened."

"Well, the whole night was kind of a mess."

"Oh, honey." Kristy rubbed Wynne's shoulder. "What happened?"

"Rolf didn't show. Evidently there was a misunderstanding, although I don't know how that was possible. Anyway, Dierk was the one who told me about Rolf, and I did as you suggested, thinking he might offer to take his brother's place."

Kristy grinned and poked her in the rib. "You like him, don't you?"

Wynne shrugged. "I do." She sighed. "But it doesn't matter. He made it absolutely clear he isn't interested."

"Oh, no." Kristy twisted her mouth into a scowl. "He's an idiot if he doesn't see what a prize you are."

"Spoken like a true best friend."

They continued to work in silence.

What was salvaged could fit in a shoebox. Kristy kept the orphaned shoe, just in case its match was found.

The box arrived just after five. It was large, brown, of a typical nondescript cardboard variety. The label had no return address.

Kristy wasn't home when it arrived. Wynne decided she'd wait until Kristy came home from work to open it. That decision lasted for all of twenty minutes. Then she said to hell with that, went to the kitchen for a knife, and sliced open the tape.

It was full of bondage stuff, absolutely brimming. At the bottom, Wynne found a small envelope, taped to a shoebox. Inside was a gray note card with a handwritten message.

To replace the things you lost last night.
My apologies,
Dierk

Once again, he had to go and prove himself a good, kind, thoughtful guy. Didn't he know what that was doing to her? Better for her if he'd be rude, an asshole, so she could shove him out of her mind, out of her dreams.

She checked the shoebox. The shoes weren't exactly like the ones she'd been wearing, but if Wynne had to guess, they were much nicer. The name on the box told her that much: Manolo Blahnik.

What the hell was this man trying to do?

Because he was Twilight's manager, Wynne could understand why he might think he should replace the things that were damaged, although even that was a stretch. But by sending all of this stuff, he'd gone way beyond what anybody would expect.

She set the shoes aside, settling on a compromise. Those were going back. The rest, she'd keep. But then, as she was showering later, she heard Kristy screeching, "Oh. My. Goddddd! He sent you Blahniks?"

Wynne mentally prepared herself for a wicked debate, knowing Kristy would think she was insane for wanting to return them.

By the time she was dressed, she was ready.

Kristy practically pounced on her the second she stepped out of the bathroom. And, of course, one of those damn pretty shoes was clutched to her chest. "They're gorgeous!"

"I'm not keeping them."

Kristy's face went pale, more like bleached sheet, reflective white. "What?"

"I can't keep them."

Kristy gaped. She really did look funny, like a dying fish beached on a dock. "Why not?"

"Because they're too expensive." Wynne tried to snatch the shoe away from her friend, but Kristy jerked it out of her reach. "Now, hand over the shoe."

"No. They're a gift." Kristy shook the shoe at her, stiletto pointing out. "You're allowed to accept expensive gifts from men. You're single. Ohmygod, they're so prettyyyyy."

"Yeah, but I don't accept costly presents from men who don't want anything to do with me." She tried for the second time to get the shoe out of Kristy's hand. This time, thanks to the fact that Kristy was too bewitched by the item in question to react, she succeeded. "I don't get this guy."

"Maybe you misunderstood. Maybe he likes you, but he doesn't know how to show you. Guys are like that sometimes."

Wynne shook her head. "Kristy, he grimaces when we get near each other, he does everything he can to avoid touching me, and he told me we could not scene again, ever. Doesn't exactly sound like true love, does it?" She headed out to the living room to get the box of bondage gear.

"Hmmmm." Kristy eyed the box. "And yet he goes out of his way to send you all this stuff."

"Because he's the manager of the club and I was almost killed. I'm sure he's trying to avoid a lawsuit."

"You think?"

"The more I think about it, the more I'm convinced that must be it. There couldn't be any other reason."

"I don't know."

"Please, *please*, agree with me." Holding the heavy box, she gave Kristy a pointed look. "I need to believe he did this for some rational reason. Or I'm going to go crazy, trying to figure him out."

Kristy nodded. "Yes, you must be right. He's afraid you're going to sue him for negligence."

"Yes. Negligence. There wasn't a light. It was very dark. Extremely dangerous."

Kristy nodded again. "Yes, that's a very serious issue. He'd better get a light put back there pronto, before someone gets hurt."

Wynne smiled, though she didn't feel happy at all. Nor relieved. Just confused and frustrated. "Thanks, sweetie."

"You're welcome." Kristy grabbed one side of the box, to help her. They shuffled down the narrow hallway toward Wynne's bedroom. "Hey, when're you headed back to Twilight?"

"Rolf called," Wynne said over the box. "He rescheduled for tomorrow night."

"Excellent!"

Wynne smiled as she dropped the heavy load onto the bed. The contents clanked and rattled. "At least I'll have a well-stocked kit."

Kristy sat on the bed and dug through the box, lifting a pair of thick leather wrist restraints. "He's going to put you through hell with all this stuff."

"Is that a good thing or bad?"

Kristy's expression was undeniably wicked. "Most definitely good."

11

Unlike last night, tonight Master Rolf was waiting for Wynne the moment she stepped through Twilight's front door. He pretty much ambushed her the second her foot crossed the threshold. "I heard what happened! Are you okay?" Taking her hand, Rolf gave her a long, scrutinizing up and down look.

"I'm fine. Didn't get a single scratch, thanks to your brother." She did a little turn to let him see she was 100 percent injury-free.

"It was damn good he was out there." Evidently convinced she was okay, he took her duffle bag and started toward the dungeon.

"Yes," she agreed. "It was no less than a miracle." She motioned toward the bag. "A lot of the things you bought for me were ruined, but Master Dierk replaced them and added a lot more. I think he's feeling a little guilty."

"Oh really?" That seemed to surprise Rolf, which, in turn, stunned her. Surely Dierk's own brother knew what a caring man he was, how honorable and generous and kind.

"I guess he figured, since he's the manager, he was somewhat responsible," she reasoned, intentionally avoiding the mention of the shoes.

"Sure, that must be it." The corner of Rolf's mouth twitched. Turning around, he continued through the dungeon and out into the hallway leading to the private suites. He let them into his suite and Wynne presented, as she'd been taught, waiting for Rolf to tell her what to do next.

"Undress." He took her kit to the raised table and began searching through the contents.

While he checked out her new gear, she removed her clothing, folded it, set it in a neat pile on a nearby chair, and returned to her position.

"This way." He motioned toward a piece of furniture that looked like a two-sided bench. The horizontal kneeling surfaces were slanted slightly, angling down toward a raised, padded center beam. The beam's sides angled out a little, reminding Wynne of a saddle stand. It was narrow enough for her legs to fit around it, but wide enough to support her bottom.

When Rolf walked toward her, he held a vibrator in his hands. Clearly, he had some more orgasm control training in mind.

Kristy's words echoed in her ears. *He's going to put you through hell with all this stuff.* Wasn't that the truth. Kristy had known all too well how fiendish Rolf could be. There were quite a number of tools in that bag that could deliver downright painful lessons. Wynne was hoping he'd stick with the ones that would produce more pleasant sensations today.

"I sanitize this after every use. Down here." He patted the top of the horse, near one end. "I want you lying face down, legs resting on the side supports."

She swung up and took the position he described, back up, bottom toward him, pubic bone resting on the very edge of the cushion, knees bent, legs supported by the slanted side supports.

It was a very sexy position, making her feel vulnerable and exposed. Her pussy started to thrum, her inner walls clenching as she closed her eyes and imagined Dierk standing behind her, holding that vibrator.

"Whatever is said between us is kept between us, Wynne. There is no reason to keep secrets from me."

"The cameras?" she pointed toward the visible equipment, mounted in the room's corner.

"Off." He dragged the vibe down her spine, little humming vibrations buzzing through her back.

"What do you want me to tell you, Master? What do you want to know?"

He moved the vibrator up, slowly, drawing lazy circles on the back of her neck. Little shivers skittered up and down her limbs. "All of your secrets. Every one of them, starting with who you think about as you masturbate." He whispered. "What face do you see when you close your eyes and touch yourself?"

"M-Master Dierk's."

"As I suspected." He slid the vibe down her side, skirting around the outer swell of a flattened breast. "Close your eyes now. Picture him."

"Yes, Master."

"You are under his control, powerless to escape. But even if you could, you wouldn't want to, would you?"

"N-no."

"You're shaking from the need for his touch, his kiss, his dick thrusting inside your wet pussy."

"Yes." She rocked her hips forward, rubbing her aching groin against the leather. She bent her legs more, pulling her knees up toward her shoulders. "Yes."

"He wants you, but he can't have you. You're his temptation, his weakness. He must fight his need." Something touched her bottom. Hard. Vibrating. She shuddered and arched her back.

"Dierk, take me, please."

The hard thing, the vibrator's tip, found her clit, and a burst of erotic need shot through her body. She went instantly hot, tight, and breathless, for one, two, three seconds.

Then it was gone and she dragged in a deep breath.

Rolf teased her with the toy again, but just like last time, it wasn't the buzzing, zapping sensation that was sending her blood pumping and heart racing, it was his words. "You torture him, Wynne, with your sweet face and wicked little body. Your tits. He aches to pull on those pink nubs. Feel them harden on his tongue. He can smell your need, and he draws in the scent, desperate for more. He hungers for a taste of your honey, the nectar like a gift from the gods. He needs to eat it away, to push his fingers into your slick pussy, to test your tight passage."

She could see Dierk doing all those things, could feel him. It wasn't a plastic toy circling her hot pussy; it was his fingers. And she was going to die if he didn't take her now.

The touches stopped. She lay panting and tight and in agony, waiting for him to return. Up above her head, on the opposite end of the long horse, she heard something. She glanced up and through need-fogged eyes watched Rolf strap a thick dildo to the horse, positioning it straight up.

"Ride his cock," Rolf demanded.

She was all too eager to obey. She sat up, straddled the dong, and slowly lowered herself onto it. Her breath left her in one drawn-out moan.

She curled the fingers of one hand into a fist, and bracing it against the horse's padded top, used it to balance herself as she raised and lowered herself onto the rubber dong. With the other, she stroked her clit, quick, little circles, eager to reach release.

It didn't take long, not with the image of Dierk playing in her mind. He was lying on his back and she was straddling his hips, not wood and leather and padding, and she was slamming down on him, his cock filling her so perfectly she had to grit her teeth against the temptation to scream his name.

"Don't come," he whispered. "Not until I tell you to."

She felt her body go tight all over. She was close, so close. She dragged her fingernails down his chest, raking the smooth, tanned flesh.

He moaned, and she joined him, throwing her head back as she fought against her body.

"Don't come."

She clenched her knees, locking them against his hips, and stilled. Her pussy twitched around his hard cock. She sucked in a breath, two, jammed her fingers through her hair and squeezed her eyelids tighter.

He was such a cruel Master, denying her what she'd waited for, needed, for so long.

"Please, Master." She tightened her inner muscles, imagining his eyes going dark with hard, male need.

"You may begin again."

This time, she was determined to find release.

Letting herself be carried away by her fantasy, she vowed to drive him crazy so he couldn't stop her. She rode him hard, bending over and flattening her tits against his slick, hard chest. Her racing heartbeat pounded in her ears. Her hands trembled. Her body quaked. She ground against him hard, rubbing her pussy against his groin, the delicious friction sending wave upon wave of erotic heat blazing up her chest.

"Do not come," he repeated, sensing she was close again.

"Bastard," she whispered.

"Do not come." His voice was sharper.

She reached back and fingered her anus, dragging some of her cream back to lubricate it. "Will you fuck me here, Master?"

"Do. Not. Come."

She pushed the tip of her finger into her anus. "Oooooh!" She squeezed her thighs and froze, unable to move a single muscle, not even to breathe. If she did, she knew she would come, and Dierk would be displeased, and she so wanted to please him. So, so badly.

"Now." His voice was hoarse, gritty.

She pushed her finger deeper, and a light flashed behind her closed eyelids. A deep tingle erupted into a whole-body spasm.

"Sparrow," he shouted, just as the spasm took hold of her. "Sparrow."

She quaked and moaned and shook and shivered, completely lost in a tempest of ecstasy. She enjoyed every beautiful second until slowly the sensations eased, the heat cooled, the spasms gentled, and her mind cleared.

She opened her eyes.

She was alone. On top of her clothes, she found a note, succinct and emotionless and a tiny bit unsettling.

Master Zane.
Next Friday. Eight P.M.
If you wish.
Master Rolf

Friday night, Wynne sat in her car and checked the clock for the third time. Seven fifty-eight. She had two minutes to decide. Should she? Or shouldn't she?

She'd spent the last six days and nights recalling every minute of her session with Rolf. Truth be told, she couldn't stop thinking about it, about how real he'd made it for her. She'd heard Dierk's voice. Felt his caresses. Smelled that intoxicating scent that came from only him.

What was it about him that stirred her so deeply? And why, oh why, was she allowed to have him only in her imagination?

This sucked. In the worst way.

She shook her head. That sounded way too much like the beginnings of a pity party for her liking. She gritted her teeth, nodded her head, and scooped up her bag. That was it. This girl did not hold pity parties under any circumstances.

She headed inside the building, checked in, and walked through the dungeon. It was a busy night at Twilight. There were groups of people clustered around the Saint Andrew's Cross, the bondage table, and the cage in the corner. In the center, a woman was tied in an intricate web of ropes, balanced on one leg with her arms tightly bound to her body. Wynne hesitated in order to watch for just a moment, intrigued but afraid to stick around too long. She was already late for her session with Zane. Some form of punishment was sure to come.

Fascinating. She decided she wanted to try that rope bondage sometime. Shibari. She'd read a little about it. But she didn't want to try it with just anyone; she would wait. Until she'd found the perfect Master.

She hurried on, fully aware of every second that ticked by. When she finally stepped into Master Zane's suite, she knew she was in trouble.

Master Zane was sitting on the couch, his long legs stretched out in front of him, one arm thrown over the sofa's back. If not for the flogger in his hands and the dangerous look on his face she would have thought he was simply sitting there relaxing. Their gazes met and a little quiver of excitement shimmied up her spine.

She had never realized she was such a glutton for punishment, in the most literal sense.

Immediately, she dropped her gaze. "Master, I apologize for being late."

"Undress. Leave on the G-string."

She started stripping off her clothes.

"You will never be late again."

"Yes, Master."

As soon as she had her clothing off, he ordered her to the wall. She went quickly, hoping to appease him, turned to face the wall, and extended her arms out to the sides. Her breathing quickened as each wrist and ankle was bound.

"Tonight you'll get a taste of my wrath."

Her heart skipped a beat. Maybe two. Nervous energy tangled her insides into knots. "Please, forgive me, Master. Please."

"What a pretty plea, coming from a pretty mouth, a pretty face, a pretty little slave." His voice was even, hollow, icy.

Wynne heard the leather thump on her back before she felt the pain. A tiny fraction of a moment later, sharp stinging pain gripped her, searing along her spine.

Too much.

"Please, Master. Not so hard. Yellow."

"Is this better?" He struck her again, and more pain—no less severe than the first time—sliced through her body.

Tears instantly sprang to her eyes, and she cried out, "Red. Red!"

This was more than she'd bargained for, way too intense. When he released her, she practically crumpled to the floor, clapped her hands over her face, and cried. To her surprise, he held her tenderly, whispering words she was sobbing too loudly to hear. When she was finally able to stop, she uncovered her face, finding a very different-looking Zane kneeling beside her.

Ever so gently, he wiped her tears from her face with his hand.

"I'm sorry," she sputtered, her voice still shaky. "I don't think I'm the right submissive for you."

Master Zane nodded and helped her to her feet. "It's okay." He helped her to the couch. While she rested, he gathered her clothes and handed them to her. Then he sat, his gaze politely averted, and waited for her to redress.

Just before she left, she touched his arm. "You taught me something about myself. Thanks for that."

"You're welcome." He gave her a hint of a smile. "I hope you find what you're looking for."

"Me, too."

She stepped out into the hall and shut the door behind her, knowing he was right. She'd started this journey thinking she was headed in one direction, but now she was going in another. She still wasn't absolutely positive what she was doing here, or what she was hoping for. But she could say one thing for sure: what she needed wasn't what Master Zane had to offer.

"Wynne."

Dierk?

She spun around, finding he was standing no more than a few feet away. His jaw was clenched, his fingers curled into tight fists.

"Is something wrong?" she asked. "I've been meaning—"

"This way." He caught her elbow and tugged her toward the end of the hall.

Something inside her snapped. "What is your problem?" She yanked her arm out of his grip and dug in her heels. This hot and cold game was getting really annoying. She would've had enough even if she wasn't edgy after that session with Zane. As it was, she wasn't in the condition to deal with any crap, from anyone.

He spun around and thrust his arms forward, caging her head between them. His gaze drilled into hers. "Tell me you won't scene with that bastard again. I warned you about him."

He was pushing her buttons at the wrong time.

She glared right back at him. "What's it to you, Dierk?" When he didn't answer, her blood spiked even hotter. She shoved at his chest but he didn't back off, so she just kept hitting it, punctuating each sentence with a smack. "You're. A.

Bastard. Sending all kinds of mixed signals, telling me one thing and then doing another. I've had enough. E-nough. Fucking tell me what the hell you're thinking, because I am going crazy trying to guess. Tell. Me."

He jerked away. "I'm sorry."

She waited for several seconds, thinking he was going to offer some kind of explanation. When he didn't, she saw all kinds of red. And it wasn't a pretty sight. "That's it? That's all you're going to say?"

He shook his head. "I don't know what else to say."

"I could make some suggestions." This time, she was the one pulling on his arm. "Let's go to your suite and have a little talk, shall we?" She felt his muscles harden under her touch. She guessed he wasn't used to having a little subby talk to him this way, but she was at her wits' end. She wasn't leaving Twilight tonight without speaking her piece.

She'd give him privacy; that was the only concession she was going to make. And that was only for the sake of his career. Otherwise, it was all guns blazing.

She'd let this go on long enough.

Once the door was shut, she screwed her face into the meanest glare she could muster, crossed her arms over her chest, and asked, "So, I'm going to listen and you're going to talk. I want to know why you're practically seducing me one minute, then acting cold and aloof the next?"

He looked a little like a kid caught standing next to a broken window, holding a baseball. He was visibly tense, from his forehead to his legs. His hands were still clenched in fists. The arteries on his arms bulged. "I'm trying to . . . I haven't . . ." He shook his head. "I find you incredibly attractive, but I can't get involved. Not with you or anyone." As she watched, some of the tension eased from his body.

It took a few seconds for his words to sink in, since she'd been more focused on his body language than what he was saying. He had actually admitted he was attracted to her. Now, she was the one having a difficult time finding the right words. "Okay."

"You're beautiful." He started to lift one hand but then dropped it again. "You're intelligent. Incredibly intuitive. You smell amazing." A hint of a smile spread over his face. "And I am captivated by the mixture of sweet vulnerability and tough independence I see in you. I'm not the only one, but I'm assuming you know that."

She'd never heard anyone describe her the way Dierk had just now, which made it that much more disappointing that he didn't believe he could pursue something with her. "You can't . . . ?"

He shook his head. "There's no way. It wouldn't be fair to you."

"Not even a session every now and then? What if we were to scene in the main dungeon?"

"I don't think that would be a good idea." He looked away for the first time since they'd entered his suite. "If you aren't comfortable with Rolf, I could introduce you to some other Doms I know."

A little chill skittered up her spine. "Did Rolf say something to you about me?"

"No." Dierk looked her straight in the eye. "Not a word. But I know something happened the last time you two scened. I saw him afterward and he wasn't acting like himself."

Now it was her turn to feel like an ass.

This bondage stuff was really complicated. On the surface, the casual relationships, experimenting, exploring, all sounded healthy, good. But the reality was, people's feelings were getting involved and what was meant to be casual, no-strings-attached play wasn't ending that way.

"On no." She slumped onto a nearby chair and covered her face with her hands. "I need some time to think about this. Maybe I should take a break from Twilight for a few weeks."

"I'm not suggesting you've done anything wrong."

"No, I know you're not. I'm just not sure this environment is right for me." She sighed, curled her fingers, and raked them through her hair. "Maybe I need something different, a committed type of relationship."

He chewed on his thumbnail for a second, then scrubbed at his stubbly jaw. "Again, I'm sorry for sending mixed signals. I've never had such a difficult time. . . . I . . . care about you."

She gazed deeply into his eyes, and her heart lurched. They were so dark, so full of regret. "I think I get it." She stood, opened the door, and turned. "Thank you for being honest."

He nodded. "You're welcome."

She left.

That was that.

12

"Ohmygod, do I know you?" Standing in the hallway outside of their apartment, Kristy winked and pushed a brown paper bag into Wynne's hands. "I bought you a gift."

"A gift? What did I do to deserve this?"

"Absolutely nothing. Heck, I haven't seen you in days. You've all but abandoned me. But I saw this, and I just knew I had to buy it for you."

"What did you buy?" Intrigued, Wynne plunged her hand into the bag. But before she pulled out what she had curled her fingers around, Kristy stopped her.

Kristy tipped her head toward the apartment door, still closed and locked. "Better get inside first."

More curious than she had been before, Wynne released the item from her clutch, dug out her keys, unlocked the door, and only after the two of them were safely inside did she reach into the bag again.

When she withdrew her fist, she saw instantly why Kristy had suggested she wait. "Is this what I think it is?"

"Your very own remote control vibrator," Kristy said,

snatching the package out of her hand. "I have one just like it, and I can't tell you how—"

"Please stop! T. M. I. It's bad enough you bought this for me. I don't want to hear what you do with yours." Wynne opened the bag and with a tip of her head, indicated Kristy should place the toy in it. "Let's just put it away for now. . . ."

"You are such a prude."

"How could you say that? I've come a long way. I've been going to the dungeon regularly."

"Sure."

"And I've even played with more than one Dom."

"Yeah, *so I've heard*." Kristy gave her a weighty look as she kicked off her shoes.

Still standing just inside the door, Wynne set her purse on a nearby table and dropped her keys into it. "What? I'm not doing anything wrong, am I? They've been introducing me to each other."

"Absolutely not." Kristy donned a pout as she wandered toward the kitchen. "It's just not right that you have written me off lately."

Wynne followed her. "I'm sorry, sweetie. Do you hate me?"

"If I did, would I have bought you a present?" Kristy opened the freezer, scowled.

"No, I guess not."

Kristy shut the freezer and leaned back against the counter, crossing her ankles and arms. "Are you busy tonight?"

"Nope." Wynne decided she wouldn't go into details yet about her decision to take a break from the scene for a while.

"Good. How about a girl's night in? I want to hear all about your escapades at Twilight. Every dirty detail. Leave nothing out, especially the really bad stuff." Kristy winked.

"You are so perverted. How could I have not realized that before now?"

Kristy shrugged. "Because I put on a good act?"

"I guess so."

"So." Kristy hurried out of the kitchen, making a beeline for her huge tote sitting on the coffee table. She started digging through its contents. "Do we have a date tonight?"

"Sure."

"Good. I was hoping you'd say that." Kristy lifted her cell phone. "I'll order the food. The usual?" Kristy didn't wait for Wynne to answer before hitting the SEND button, placing a call to their favorite Thai restaurant.

"Okay." Wynne filled a couple of glasses with ice and carried them and a bottle of diet cola into the living room. She set them on the coffee table.

As Kristy placed their order, Wynne went back to her bedroom, shoved the paper bag and its contents into her underwear drawer, and changed into a comfy pair of sweats and a T-shirt. By the time she returned to the living room, Kristy was on the couch, feet kicked up, remote in hand.

"The food's being delivered," Kristy told her. "I didn't feel like driving over to pick it up. Please tell me you TiVo'd the season premier of *Rock of Love Five*."

"You know I did! How could I miss that train wreck?"

"Good!"

They watched no more than three minutes before Kristy started, "Okay, I've waited long enough. How're things going at Twilight?"

Wynne acted all casual, giving a slight shrug. "It's going pretty good, I guess. I've been having fun."

"I hear your name there quite a bit. There's talk among the Doms."

The casual act completely abandoned, she twisted to face Kristy. "About me? What kind of talk?"

"They all want you."

Wynne felt her cheeks heating up. She pursed her lips and snatched up a throw pillow, hugging it to her chest. "That's weird. I'm so new. I can't handle the stuff I see other submissives doing."

Kristy shrugged. "They say there's something about you. What's interesting to me is the reaction I see from Master Dierk whenever your name is brought up." Wynne's heart did a little jump, and Kristy gave Wynne a probing look and nudge with her elbow. "Is there something up between you two?"

Wynne hugged the pillow tighter. "No. I mean, we played once, but that's as far as it's gone."

"I get a sense he's uncomfortable with you scening with other Doms, especially Master Zane. His face turns ten shades of red whenever he hears your name mentioned with Zane's. And I'm noticing something between Dierk and his brother, too, a little bit of tension. I think he's feeling a little protective."

She knew what Kristy was getting at, but she was wrong. "He's not being possessive over me."

"That's the only thing I can think of, with the way he's been acting. What makes you believe I'm wrong?"

"I just know."

Kristy studied her for a few minutes. "What's going on, Wynnie? You're keeping something from me."

"Well . . ." She didn't know what to say, where to start.

Kristy leaned forward. "I don't think Dierk's scened with another submissive at Twilight. Only with you."

"That's just because his brother screwed up and forgot he'd scheduled a session with me. But that's neither here nor there. I've decided to take a break from the scene for a while."

Kristy frowned. "I think you're making a mistake."

"It's not what I'm looking for. I want one man. I want him to make me feel desired, safe, protected . . . and loved . . . forever. Not for an hour, or a night, or a week."

"Wynne, are you falling in love with Dierk?"

"I . . . I don't know." Wynne dropped her chin onto the pillow and closed her eyes. "I mean, I feel something for all three of the Doms I've scened with. Master Rolf was my first, and so he's very special to me. He's so considerate during play, gentle, firm, sensual. He makes me feel sexy. And Master Zane is almost the opposite. He is super tough and demands total surrender, but that is such a huge rush sometimes."

"But . . . ?"

"But there was something different about Master Dierk, right from the moment our eyes first met. It's an energy, that's the only way I can describe it. Our exchanges are intense, magical, no matter where we are or what we're doing. And I always want more. More time. More touches. More *him*."

Kristy beamed. "I'd say that would be a yes, then."

Wynne didn't answer. There was no need to. "I'm setting myself up for heartbreak."

"Not necessarily."

"Oh, yes I am. He told me he can't pursue a relationship right now. Not with anyone."

"Why?"

"He didn't say." Wynne scrubbed her face with her flattened hands. "But he did tell me, after some arm twisting, that he is attracted to me. Actually, he said more than that. It was sweet. . . . What am I going to do?"

"Follow your heart. That's what we all do."

Wynne poured some cola into one of the glasses. "But if I do that, I'm going to get hurt." She gave Kristy a pleading look. "Tell me I'm being an idiot. Tell me he's an asshole and doesn't deserve to lick the dirt off my shoes. Don't tell me he's a good guy and I should try to find out why he can't give us a chance."

"I think he's a good guy." Kristy wrapped her arm around Wynne's shoulder and gave it a squeeze. "And I think you'll regret it forever if you don't try to find out why he's holding back. If he's really as attracted to you as you're suggesting, he owes you an explanation about why he won't give you a shot."

"How am I going to get him to do that?"

Kristy gave her a meaningful grin. "I think you know what to do."

"No, really, I don't."

A knock sounded at the door and Kristy leapt to her feet. "Food's here." Wynne set down her glass and stood, prepared to get some money from her purse, but Kristy stopped her. "Nope. It's my turn to pay. Remember? You got it last time."

"Okay. Thanks."

"My pleasure." Kristy gathered some cash from her wallet and hurried toward the door. Before she opened it, she turned to face Wynne. "You know Dierk like nobody else at Twilight does. I can't tell you what to do. You've got to figure it out for yourself. There's got to be a way to approach him, make him feel comfortable so he'll feel comfortable telling you the truth." Then she turned around, opened the door, and greeted the delivery man on the other side with a smile and a friendly, "Hey there!" She thrust the money at him and accepted the large paper bag he'd been holding in his arms. "Thanks. Keep the change." After the man thanked her, she shut the door and trotted back toward Wynne. She set the bag on the coffee table and started pulling white styrofoam cartons out of it. "So you aren't going to scene with Rolf and Zane anymore?"

"No. I told Zane I wasn't the right submissive for him during our last session. He's too . . . intense for me. And Rolf . . . not for a while, not until I find out what's going on with Dierk. And maybe not even after that. It's not right, not with Dierk being his brother."

Kristy picked up a baby corn from one of the containers and slipped it into her mouth. "Mmmm, good stuff." She licked her fingers. "I wish I could help you sort this stuff out."

"Do I need to talk to Rolf? Explain myself?"

"No. He'll understand." Kristy handed her a container.

Wynne set it on the coffee table, next to her glass of cola. "I

feel bad. I mean, I think he kind of knows, after our last session."

"Don't worry about it. He has other subs. He isn't going to
be upset."

"You're sure?"

"Positive. It happens all the time." Kristy pointed a plastic
fork wrapped in a white napkin at Wynne's nose. "If you're
asking my opinion, I think you should concentrate on Dierk."

Wynne snatched the fork. "Thanks."

She wasn't just grateful for the fork. Or the food.

"It might be easier to get him to talk if I could spend some
time with him outside of the dungeon," Wynne mumbled as
she unwrapped a spring roll.

Kristy's smile turned devious. "I think that could be
arranged."

13

"The Venus Lounge?" Wynne read the sign as Kristy turned into the parking lot and maneuvered her subcompact into the one empty parking spot in sight. Clearly, this club was popular, though she had no clue why, not from the exterior. "Sounds like a strip joint."

"That's because it is." Kristy cut off the engine.

"Oh, come on." Wynne crossed her arms over her chest. "Why did you bring me here?"

Kristy dropped her car keys into her purse and pulled out her lipstick. "Because I've heard this is one of Dierk's favorite hangouts." She checked her makeup in the rearview mirror, smiled to make sure she didn't have makeup on her teeth, then dropped the unused tube back in her purse.

"Dierk's favorite hangout is a strip club?"

"A gentleman's club," Kristy corrected. "Ready to go inside?"

Was she insane?

"We can't go in there."

"Sure we can." Kristy unbuckled her seat belt and opened

her door. "Are you staying in the car or coming with me? I'm doing this for you. You said you wanted to spend time with Dierk outside of the dungeon."

"Yeah, but I had something a little more . . ." *Normal.* ". . . low key in mind. Like maybe dinner."

"They serve incredible food here. Just because the waitresses' asses hang out of their shorts doesn't mean the place serves second-rate food."

"Yeah, well . . ." Still sitting in the car, Wynne watched her friend totter on her five-inch stilettos toward the door. "Oh hell." When Kristy disappeared into the building, Wynne stared down at her hands. She'd never been in a place like this. She imagined it would be like the seedy dumps she'd seen in movies, crowded and smoky, dark with colored lights flashing and mostly naked women on a raised stage, hips gyrating to earsplitting music. It was so far from the kind of environment she'd hoped for, not at all intimate or romantic; she couldn't imagine any reason why she should even bother going inside.

For one thing, how would she get Dierk's attention when there would be dozens of tight and tanned female bodies on display? She wasn't tight, tanned, or nude.

And that wasn't even the point.

She'd enjoyed a little quality time with Dierk in the dungeon, but that time had been spent doing things that were commonly done in a dungeon, which was fine. But the whole purpose of this visit was to see if she could hope for more.

She wanted to know Dierk. As a human being, not just a Dom. It might be silly, but she wanted to know what he ate for breakfast, what he watched on television, what he dreamed about at night. How could she learn those things while some naked girl was standing in front of him, tits bouncing to some old Judas Priest song?

What the hell had Kristy been thinking?

Annoyed, Wynne turned to look at the grungy building,

hoping Kristy had noticed by now that she was still in the car. A face appeared, not Kristy's, seemingly out of nowhere, and a shriek surged up Wynne's throat. But before it flew out, something clicked in her brain.

That was Dierk's face in the driver's side window.

While she collected herself—she'd just about peed her pants—he knocked on the glass and shouted, "Are you okay?"

She reached over and unlocked the door, waiting until he had it opened before answering, "Yes, I'm fine. You just startled me a little."

Bending at the waist, he motioned to the seat. "May I?"

"Oh, absolutely. But fair warning, it's a little cramped."

It took him a few seconds to get in; he had to move the seat as far back as it would go. Once he was settled and had the door closed, he turned to her. "Kristy told me you were out here."

"Yes." She cleared her throat. "I didn't know she was bringing me here . . . to a . . . well, nothing against places like this, but I didn't feel . . . um . . ." She couldn't say more. The right words simply weren't there, only the wrong ones, and she didn't want to sound stupid or judgmental. Or rather, more stupid or judgmental than she already sounded.

"It's okay. I understand." He smiled, and the world was pretty much right again and she didn't feel stupid anymore, only warm and happy. And hungry. "Are you hungry?" he asked.

Was he a psychic? Scary. "Oh, uh, Kristy told me they serve good food here, but—"

"No," he cut her off. "I was thinking we could go somewhere else, maybe somewhere quieter, where we could talk."

Yes!

She nodded. "I would be glad to."

"Good."

She pointed toward the bar. "But I should probably let Kristy know first."

"Already done."

"Well then. I guess you were pretty sure I'd accept your invitation."

"Not really. I told her I would offer, but if I was shot down, I'd drive you home anyway."

"How gallant," she said, pronouncing the second word with an accent on the second syllable, like her mother used to. "You're willing to take me home even if I turn down an invitation to dinner?"

"Absolutely. My car's parked around back. Wait here." After she nodded, he left.

A little giddy, she watched him jog around the side of the building. A few minutes later, a sleek black sports car prowled toward her, the motor a low hum that reverberated through her body. The car stopped next to Kristy's and no sooner did Wynne have her door open than Dierk was at her side, guiding her into his car's low, black leather seat.

She felt like the soft leather cradled her when she sat, and she noticed, as Dierk walked around the front, that the vehicle's interior smelled really good, like new car and Dierk.

He drove fast, which wasn't such a surprise, considering what he was driving, but she wasn't nervous. He proved within a few short miles, when a little white Saturn shot out in front of them, that he had lightning-quick reflexes, steering out of what would have been a fatal accident before Wynne had even realized what was happening.

Yes, just like she did in the dungeon, she felt safe with Dierk, protected. And wonderfully excited. Every time she looked at him, he was more handsome. And she knew those good looks weren't wasted on a self-centered, hedonistic bastard either.

"I'm glad you came to the club tonight," Dierk said shortly after the close call with the Saturn. He maneuvered his car into a tiny gap in the heavy traffic on the freeway.

"Ironically, so am I."

They exchanged a smile. "That was Raven's idea, bringing me there," she added.

He nodded, signaled, and changed lanes. "She told me." After a beat, he asked, "Which do you prefer, steak or Italian?"

"Either is fine."

"That's not what I asked."

"You're going to make me choose?" When he gave her a pointed look, she laughed. "Okay, how about steak?"

"Good choice." He punched the gas and cut across three lanes of traffic, making it into the right lane just in time to exit the highway.

Miraculously, she didn't brace herself against the dash. "You know, if it would have been easier to get to the Italian restaurant, I would've said that."

"Which is why I didn't mention it."

She laughed again, and this time Dierk joined her. It wasn't a hearty, belly-busting guffaw, more a nervous chuckle, but it felt good releasing some of that jittery energy.

She couldn't help noticing that laughter did something magical to Dierk's face. He hadn't laughed in the dungeon, so this was the first she'd seen it. His eyes lit up—no, his whole being did. A face that was already remarkable became impossibly more amazing.

"Have you read that book I gave you yet?"

Her cheeks warmed. *Busted.* "I've read part of it. I've been busy lately, haven't had much time for reading."

"What do you think so far?"

"It's very fast-paced, a genuine page-turner. Tight and suspenseful. I find myself wanting to keep reading, even when I need to stop."

He nodded as he checked the rearview mirror. "It gets better." He changed lanes and hit the right turn signal.

"If that's the case, I'm in trouble. I'd better make sure I can set aside some time before I pick it up again."

"Good idea." He turned the car into a parking lot. While he pulled into an empty spot, she checked the sign. She'd never heard of this restaurant. "I know the owner. You'll love the food here."

"I can't wait."

He twisted toward her then and her heart did a little bunny hop in her chest. He was staring at her mouth, and she couldn't breathe. Was he going to kiss her? How many times had she wished he would? At least a million. Maybe even a billion.

He reached for her, ran a fingertip down the side of her face, and a little quiver of expectation shot through her. His eyes found hers. He leaned closer. Closer still. She closed her eyes, sure he was about to kiss her. Finally!

"You smell good," he murmured in her ear. A soft current of air caressed her neck and goose bumps puckered all over the left side of her body. A tingly warmth ignited low, between her legs. She squeezed them together and relaxed fingers that had been curled around the edge of the seat, fingernails digging into the supple hide.

Still, there was no kiss. But that tickly stream of air continued, like the softest touch, slowly traveling down her neck to the crook of her collarbone. She had to force herself to inhale. Her head was spinning.

"Dierk?"

"I want to taste you but I don't dare. Because if I do, I know I won't want to stop." His hand moved back, fingers sliding into her hair at her temple then curling.

"I wouldn't want you to stop either."

"Mmmmm." He pulled, gently coaxing her to tip her head to one side. He closed the other hand around her neck. He didn't use any pressure on her throat, so air could move in and out freely, or at least it should have. But because her body was tightening all over, it couldn't. She gasped.

He put a little pressure on the underside of her chin, forcing it up. Something came closer to her mouth, something warm. Something that smelled really good. But in less than a heartbeat it was gone, and so were his hands.

No kiss.

"Wait here." Before she responded, he opened his door and walked around the car to get hers. Like the perfect gentleman he always played, he helped her out. But going above and beyond, he held her hand as they walked across the parking lot and into the building.

They were seated immediately, despite the crush of people in the lobby area waiting for tables. They were led to a room sectioned off from the main dining area. Empty, quiet, and private. Their table was set in the rear, in a cozy corner. A candle flickered on the table, creating a soft, wavering light that made what was already a romantic setting even more so.

Once they'd taken care of ordering drinks and appetizers, and the waiter had hustled off, Dierk rested his elbows on the table, steepled his fingers under his chin, and gazed into her eyes. "Raven told me you needed to talk. What's on your mind?"

"Nothing really," she lied.

His eyes narrowed almost imperceptibly. "You look nervous."

"Maybe that's because I am." She unfolded her napkin and smoothed it over her lap.

"Why?"

"I don't know. We aren't strangers. We've spent a little time together, and maybe I should be more comfortable with you than I am right now. You've been honest with me all along. But there's still something between us, and I'm not sure what to do about it. With the other Doms, it was all about sensation, domination, submission, power, and surrender." She took a sip from her water glass, appreciating the chill as it slid down her throat and settled in her stomach. "But . . ."

"But what? That isn't enough for you."

Now that wasn't a question. It was a statement, a very weighted, carefully enunciated one.

"Is it enough for you?" She held her breath, hoping he would say no, praying he would sweep her into his arms and tell her he was falling in love with her and he couldn't fight it any longer.

He shook his head. "It doesn't matter what I want. What matters is what you need."

"It's not that I'm expecting anyone to drop on his knee and beg me to marry him. I'm not asking for any heavy commitment. I just want . . . need . . . more than role playing."

"Who said that's what I did with you?"

"Then you weren't? Dierk, please tell me what's going on?" He looked away, turning his profile to her, and allowing her to see he'd clenched his jaw. He was a guy, and men weren't the best at talking about feelings. She understood that. But still she wished he could say what he was thinking, feeling right now. Was he annoyed? Angry? Confused or frustrated? "When I first came to Twilight," she continued, "I was searching for answers."

"To what questions?"

"Why people went to bondage dungeons, what would drive them to seek out Doms to humiliate them, whip them, bind them. Why they would create a connection between pain and humiliation and sexuality."

Still staring off to the side, he nodded. "Yes, you said you were doing research for a book."

"You never believed that story, did you?"

The corner of his mouth twitched. "No. I've heard that story one time too many to believe it anymore."

The waiter came, drinks and appetizer balanced on a tray, and the conversation halted.

It was Dierk who started the discussion again, after the

waiter had left and they'd both taken a taste of their drinks. "Did you find your answers?"

"Yes."

"Good."

She could see he'd closed up more than he had been only a few minutes ago. He wasn't going to open up to her. Regardless, or maybe hoping it would make him relax a little, she admitted, "But now I have more questions than I had when I started, and I'm . . . I long for a closer connection, something more than physical."

"Yes, I see that."

"I don't think I'll be coming back to Twilight. At least not for a while."

He emptied his glass in a series of long gulps, then set it on the table. "You need to do what's best for you."

The waiter entered again, this time with their dinners. The conversation didn't start up again after he left. It would have been easy for Wynne to tell herself that it was because they were eating. But she knew it wasn't. First, Dierk didn't seem to be eating at all, just emptying his glass fast enough that the waiter was bringing him drinks two at a time. And second, because she would have gladly stopped eating to talk, if Dierk had looked a little more open to continuing their discussion.

The fact was, she'd dragged them into territory Dierk wasn't willing to explore. She couldn't begin to guess why. But it was what it was, and he wasn't trying to deceive her. He'd had some weak moments, but she couldn't fault him for that. Not when he'd managed to keep from even kissing her. They'd discussed the nature of their relationship before their one and only time in the dungeon. And again, he'd told her he wasn't able to pursue anything with her after her close call outside Twilight.

She wanted to keep prodding him for a more substantial explanation but she was beginning to feel whiny and clingy.

Which meant one of two things. Either she needed to somehow convince herself that friendship with him was enough, or she needed to sever the ties with him completely, hoping that would allow her to find someone else who was ready to travel the road to love with her.

If only she'd had the same feelings for Rolf or Zane as she did for Dierk. But she didn't, and there wasn't anything she could do about it.

If it couldn't be Dierk, it couldn't be any of them.

Her appetite was shot for the rest of the night.

She went home with a heavy heart and a carton full of steak, loaded baked potato, and salad. And she was as clueless as before about why Dierk was holding back.

That was not the outcome she'd hoped for.

14

"Wynne's here," Rolf announced as he strolled into Dierk's office.

Scowling, Dierk punched the ENTER button on his computer. The damn thing wasn't running right. Again. "She is?"

"Yeah. Why do you sound so surprised about that?"

"No reason." Dierk swallowed an expletive and reached down to manually power down the computer.

"Looks like you could use a break from that. Want to take my appointment with Wynne? I don't think she'd complain."

Dierk hit the POWER button, hoping the damn machine would start back up. "Nope. I won't be scening with her again."

"Does she know this yet?"

"Yes." Frustrated about more than the computer, Dierk glanced up. "I told her before the first session and again afterward."

Rolf gave him a funny look. "You're sure?"

"Positive." He looked at the monitor, hit ENTER a couple more times. Still nothing, dammit.

"Okay." Rolf headed for the door, but before he left, he turned around. "Did . . . something happen between you two? I know you're engaged and this thing with Wynne could only go so far. But it was beginning to look like—"

"No. I'm just busy, and I think it's better if I keep my personal life apart from this place."

After a long silence, Rolf nodded. "I see."

Dierk fought with the virus-riddled computer for several more hours before finally giving up. By then, he'd vented all his frustration on the machine and was ready to head out to someplace loud where there'd be plenty of distraction. The last thing he needed was quiet. He didn't want to think, didn't want to relive those moments with Wynne last night, when the candlelight had been flickering in her eyes.

Dammit. No woman had invaded his mind like that one. Not even close. And he'd had hundreds, thousands of submissives, so many he'd lost count decades ago. For some reason, Wynne's face was etched in his memory, burned there like a brand, and no matter how hard he tried—and tried he had—he couldn't erase it. He saw that face every time he closed his eyes, even when he slept. It haunted him in his dreams.

When he was away from her, he could think about nothing else. He ached to see her, to hear her voice, to smell her. And when he was close to her, all he wanted was to taste her. To pull her essence inside and have it fill him. Even that wouldn't be enough. He knew it.

He needed to possess her, make her his as only his kind could. But that could never happen. There were a couple of huge hurdles standing in his way, and there was no way he could clear either one of them.

Which meant there was no way in hell he could step inside a dungeon with her again. He couldn't trust himself to see her, talk to her, let alone touch her. If he did, there was no telling what he might do.

He couldn't imagine the consequences.

With dark thoughts for company, he waved at the head of security, letting him know he was leaving for the night, and headed out into the dark parking lot.

A sweet scent drifted to his nose, carried by a gentle evening breeze.

She was out there.

Instantly his body hardened. His cock surged to a full, painful erection. He didn't have to search hard to find her; she was standing only a hundred yards away.

She wasn't alone. Someone was touching her, holding her, maybe even kissing her. His blood chilled for an instant and then spiked hotter than acid.

He charged toward her, fury tearing through his body. His hands clenched into fists, his muscles pulled tight, preparing for battle. His eyes sharpened, adjusting to the darkness.

Rolf. She was with his brother Rolf.

Dierk halted, twisting around to hide behind an SUV. With any luck, she hadn't seen him coming yet. Her eyes wouldn't be as keen as his in the darkness.

Fuck, this was hard.

Her scent was stronger now, and he couldn't help dragging in a deep lungful. How delicious she would taste. How delightful it would feel to have her soft body molded to his, her curves pressed against his hard planes.

No, he couldn't think about that now.

He pressed his head back against the vehicle behind him and covered his face with his hands, trying to block that glorious scent from reaching his nose. If he'd been stronger, he would have walked away. But he wasn't and he couldn't. So, thanks to his weakness, he had to stand there and try not to draw in her intoxicating aroma, try to resist the sound of her sweet voice, a mesmerizing siren's song, until he could gain control of his body again.

"I'm sorry I said something now," he heard her say. Her voice was full of regret.

Dierk was sorry, too, but not because of anything she'd said or done. He was sorry he heard hurt and confusion in her voice.

"My brother has had his problems, but he would never intentionally hurt a woman."

"I believe you," she said.

"Maybe, like you said, it would be best if you didn't come here for a while," Rolf suggested.

Yes, that would be best, Dierk agreed.

"I guess you're right," she said. "I felt like I owed you an explanation."

"You don't owe me anything. Call me if you need me," Rolf offered.

Once again jealousy turned Dierk's blood to acid. *If she needs him.* The thought made Dierk's stomach clench, even though he knew Rolf was being kind. The problem was he knew how Rolf felt about her, how close he was to falling in love with her. That made this whole thing that much worse, for all of them.

He had no right to keep them apart, and yet that was exactly what he was doing. The sad truth was his heart had marked her, even though he had no right to act upon his claim.

He felt like such a shit.

How the hell was he going to get over her?

"I don't know what's worse: when you're gone all the time and forget I exist, or when you're locking yourself up in this apartment and living like a hermit." Kristy gave Wynne the pout to end all pouts. "Come on, let's go out and have some fun. I promise I won't drag you to a strip club again."

"I'm busy." Wynne lifted the book she was pretending to

read, which just happened to be the one Dierk had given her at the bookstore. "I promised someone I would read this book—"

"A book? That's bullshit." Kristy snatched the novel away, tossed it across the room, and glared at her. "Something's wrong. Tell me."

"Hey! That's a signed first edition. I can't believe you just threw it." She stomped past her annoying friend to reclaim her book. "Outside of you being a pain in the butt, nothing's wrong." She found the abused novel lying on the floor behind a chair. There didn't seem to be any damage, other than a little wrinkle on one corner of the cover. She smoothed it down.

"I've told you, you're the world's worst liar. You've been moping around here since the night you went out with Dierk. What happened? Why won't you tell me?"

"I have not been *moping*."

"Shall I look up the definition for you?"

"That won't be necessary, thank you."

Kristy, being the smart-ass she was, went to her laptop, typed in the word, and hit a button. "Mope. To move around slowly and aimlessly. To be apathetic, gloomy, or dazed. Yep, I'd say that's a dead-on description of you lately."

"Okay, okay." Wynne snapped the book shut. There was no use pretending she was reading. They both knew she wasn't. How could she, when all she could think about was a certain Dom. "I was waiting, hoping . . ."

"What?"

"I think I blew it with Dierk." She sighed. "Correction, I *know* I blew it with Dierk."

"Finally." Kristy's expression changed in a blink, from I-was-right to I'm-so-sorry. She plopped onto the couch beside Wynne and wrapped an arm around her shoulder. "Talk to me. Why didn't you tell me before?"

"I don't know. I guess I was trying not to think about it, and

I knew talking about it, about him, would make me think . . ." Wynne sighed again. It hurt to think about him. A lot. "We were never a couple. We didn't make any kind of promise or commitment to each other, and our relationship—it's a stretch to even call it that—was based solely on role playing. Still, it hurts." Wynne stared down at the book still clenched in her hands. She smoothed her palms over the cover. "I guess he played his part too well."

"Oh honey."

"That night we went out . . . I told him I wasn't looking just for a Dom, I wanted more. I didn't specifically say I wanted more from *him*, but I think he figured that out. I was hoping he'd tell me what was holding him back but he didn't. All he did was tell me I needed to do what was best for me. The next night, when I went to the dungeon, I told his brother Rolf everything. Rolf didn't offer any insight either. All he suggested was that I stay away from Twilight for a while, if that might make it easier for me."

"That was a couple of weeks ago."

She felt her shoulders slumping forward. "It feels like it's been forever."

"Of course it does." Kristy gave her shoulder another squeeze. "I wish I could do or say something to make you feel better. I have heard he isn't playing at Twilight. Not with anyone."

Wynne couldn't say whether that made her feel better or worse. Both, maybe.

After a minute or two, Kristy cleared her throat. "I heard about another dungeon opening up. The grand opening is in a couple of weeks, and of course, attendance is by invitation only. I've heard it's going to be very exclusive."

Another dungeon? Wynne's mood sank even lower. "I don't know, Kristy. If anything, this thing with Dierk has taught me that the casual bondage play stuff isn't for me."

"Hey, not all Doms are commitment phobic. In fact, a lot of them are in stable relationships. A relationship with a Dom can be really intense because of the level of trust you have to share."

Wynne shook her head. "I'm sure." The thought of starting a relationship with anyone but Dierk made her feel a little hollow inside. She honestly didn't want to talk about it, think about it, and she sure didn't want to go tromping off to another dungeon to be scoped out by other Doms. "But I'm not ready to go Dom-hunting right now."

"No, I can see you're not. I'm not going to try to talk you into going with me. But if you change your mind, let me know." Kristy sat forward. It looked like she was getting ready to leave.

Good.

Wynne gave Kristy the best smile she could muster. "Thanks. Heading out?"

"I was thinking about it, but I feel bad—"

"Don't feel bad. I'm fine. Really. Go, have some fun." She made a shooing motion with her hands. "You'll drive me crazy if you stick around here, hovering over me like a buzzard."

Kristy laughed. "Okay. I'll go. Buzzard, eh?" She stood, gave Wynne a very animated scowl, and headed toward her bedroom. "I think I should get another tattoo. I need a buzzard on my ass."

Now that made Wynne smile.

It had been too long. Thanks to Dierk's vow to keep work and play separate, he hadn't stepped foot in a dungeon, outside of work, in weeks. He'd never gone that long, and damned if it wasn't killing him.

As a business owner, he knew he should be worried about the new dungeon opening up in the area. Twilight's numbers weren't suffering yet, but he fully expected they would.

Yet, he was thankful to have another dungeon within driving distance. He would finally have an outlet for his darker needs. The urges had been building up, making him tense, short-tempered, and irritable.

He tucked the invitation into his tux pocket, snatched up his keys, and waved at Rolf as he headed out. Tonight was the grand opening. There'd be champagne, caviar, erotic art on display, and an exhibition featuring mild S and M. Tomorrow, he would take possession of his new private suite, and with luck, he'd find a new submissive to help him break it in.

He hoped there'd be some unfamiliar faces at tonight's event.

Just in case, he tucked a few of his cards into his pocket— not the ones associated with Twilight, but the ones he'd had printed for nights like tonight.

Nights when he was on the hunt for a new submissive.

15

"You look maah-ve-lous, darling!" Bedecked in a slinky black dress that clung to her curves, Kristy slipped her thumb and middle finger between her lips and blew, producing a shrill whistle. It was such a Kristy thing to do. "You are so hawt."

Feeling a little self-conscious, Wynne tugged at the strapless top. "What kind of woman was this thing made for? I'm not exactly small, and I don't have enough boobage to fill it. Was it made to fit a double D?"

"No worries. I have something for that." Kristy sauntered into her room, returning a second later with a set of pink silicone-filled inserts. "Here you go. Instant boobage."

Scowling, her hands full of smooshy half-boob inserts, Wynne muttered, "Gee, thanks," and headed into the bathroom to try them on for size.

Ironically, they did wonders. She just hoped they'd stay put in her strapless bra. If not . . . how embarrassing would it be to have one of those goofy-looking pink things drop out of the bottom of her dress.

"Why don't they have Velcro or something?" she asked as

she exited the bathroom, adjusting the dress she borrowed as she walked.

"They won't go anywhere. Trust me. That plastic'll stick to your skin like Saran Wrap."

"In that case, ew! I hope you washed them."

Kristy found her comment absolutely hysterical. "Of course I did, silly. Do you honestly think I would hand over what is basically dirty underwear to you?"

"No, I suppose you wouldn't."

"Okay. So are we ready to roll? You look fabulous. I look amazing. I say we're good to go." She sauntered across the living room.

Wynne followed. "Yes, I guess."

At the door, Kristy rolled her eyes. "Don't sound so excited. I didn't twist your arm."

"No, you didn't." Wynne trailed Kristy out the door. "I decided I would go all on my own, since it's going to be more of a wine and cheese gathering, instead of a whips and chains one. Even I have to admit, I've been living like a hermit for long enough."

"Exactly. You'll meet some new people and hopefully forget about you know who. . . ." Kristy gave her a weighted look. "I won't mention his name tonight. I promise."

"Thank you."

Kristy kept her word as they drove to the new dungeon, located in a very secluded but gorgeous building in a nearby town. The sun had just slipped below the horizon and the sky was painted in deep purples with smudges of pinky peach. The towering trees behind the house blocked most of the remaining light, casting the front of the house in deep shadow and chilling the air.

"This house once belonged to some rich guy in the automotive industry. Chrysler, I think," Kristy explained as they pulled into the small parking lot set off to one side. "He had to sell it after the company filed for bankruptcy." When she stepped out of the car, she sighed. "Holy shit. Could you imagine living in a place this huge? It's a freaking museum."

Wynne mirrored Kristy. "Hell no. That would be way too much work for me."

Kristy giggled. "Silly, if you could afford to live in a palace like this, you could afford to hire a couple of maids."

"Good point. Oh, and while we're dreaming, I'd hire a hot pool boy, too. Oh, and a tennis instructor with a to-die-for body. And of course they'd both work without shirts on."

"I adore your imagination. Dream on, sweetheart!" Kristy tugged on her elbow. "Shall we?"

"I guess."

They clacked across the parking lot, up the stone front steps and, after showing the man positioned at the door their invitation, stepped into the marble-tiled foyer.

"This place is insane," Wynne muttered, trying not to look like a kid wandering into Disney World for the first time. At least twenty feet above them, an enormous crystal chandelier hung, the light casting little twinkling stars all over walls reaching up to the soaring ceiling overhead. Directly in front of them stood a counter where guests would check in. Right now, there was an attractive young woman standing in front of it, handing out some kind of gift bags.

Kristy made a beeline for her and Wynne followed.

"Welcome to Il Roseto." The girl handed each of them a bag. "Inside you'll find some information about our club, as well as a special thank-you gift."

"Thanks." Wynne peered inside before stepping aside to move out of the way.

"Over here." Kristy grabbed her hand and pulled her toward a corridor. They stopped outside a set of double doors, a mass of humans creating a wall in front of them.

Wynne took the opportunity to dig into the bag.

"Holy shit, it's Dierk," Kristy whispered.

Wynne's heart stopped.

A part of her had hoped he wouldn't be here tonight, but another, the really stupid part, had hoped he would. She'd waxed and plucked and curled and primped; even she had to admit she'd never looked this good. The dress, as one would expect from a designer gown that cost the equivalent of one month's salary, emphasized the parts it should and deemphasized the parts it shouldn't. Thanks to the cut, and the Spanx she'd bought to wear under the gown, she looked like she'd lost ten pounds.

When her gaze met his, she knew all the trouble she'd gone to had been worth it. He looked like he'd seen an angel. It was almost comical. His open-mouthed stare did a great deal for her confidence until some chick—beautiful, of course—looped an arm around his and, following the line of his gaze, gave her an assessing stare.

Wynne's first thought was to leave. Right now. Before things got any more uncomfortable. In fact, she started to act on her impulse. But she stopped herself after only one step.

The world of BDSM, particularly in this region, was a small one, and she was bound to run into Dierk if she was going to be a part of it. Somehow she had to learn how to deal with it.

Chin up. You're a big girl. You can handle this. She gave the woman what she hoped was a friendly smile before turning to Kristy. "There are exactly two BDSM dungeons within a hundred-mile radius, and he runs one of them. Of course he would be here."

"Are you okay?"

"Yeah. I'll put on my happy face. I promise I won't make a scene."

"That's not the point," Kristy whispered. "If this is too hard, say the word and we're out of here."

"No, I'm not going to ruin this for you."

Kristy tipped her head and smiled. "I'm proud of you."

"Oh for chrissakes, I didn't invent the cure for cancer, I'm just dealing with an awkward situation like any mature adult would."

"Still . . ." Kristy did a double take. "Looks like he's coming this way."

"Yeah, I see that." Wynne pulled her lips back, hoping the expression would pass for a smile. "Do I look happy?"

"No, you look constipated."

"Shit." She let her face relax just before he was within arm's length. The woman, who upon closer inspection was even more perfect than she'd looked from a distance, was still draped on his arm. However, the dress she wore was a nightmare. Hideous. Wynne did her best to pretend she wasn't there. "Hello Dierk. It's good seeing you again."

"Wynne." That was all he said. He just stood there, staring at her, a blank look on his face.

Was it her imagination, or was Dierk trying to pretend that chick wasn't there, too?

"I'm Tabitha," the chick said, extending an arm. She flashed perfectly straight, blindingly white teeth.

"Oh." Dierk shook his head. "I apologize. Tabitha, this is Wynne. Wynne, Tabitha."

Wynne didn't want to shake her hand, but she did. "Nice to meet you," she muttered, trying not to bust out in a guffaw. *Where did you find that hideous dress, the Salvation Army?* "I just *love* your gown."

"Thank you." Tabitha beamed.

Wynne thought she might puke.

"We met at Twilight," Dierk explained, motioning to Wynne. "Wynne is—was—a member."

"I see." Tabitha answered with a nod.

"Yes. Twilight." Wynne wanted to say more, like how she'd

pretended Dierk had tied her up and fucked her until she came, over and over again. But she didn't. She just shook the woman's hand and turned to Kristy. "This is my friend, Mistress Raven."

"It's nice to meet you." Tabitha took Kristy's hand, gave it a shake, and released it. She patted her throat. "We were just about to get some champagne."

"Okay," Wynne said, sounding quite cheery to her own ears. The torture had gone on long enough. "Enjoy." She grabbed Kristy's arm. "We were heading into the dungeon. I see the crowd's thinning. We'd better get when the getting's good." She gave Dierk one last look then stepped around them, tugging Kristy with her. "'Bye. I'm sure we'll see you around."

"You, my dear, should be up for an Oscar for that performance," Kristy whispered in her ear.

"Really? I thought I sucked."

"Ohmygod, no. I just about lost it when you complimented her on her dress."

They shared a laugh as they strolled into the dungeon.

An angel. That was what Wynne had reminded him of tonight. That opal-hued gown, with the pleats and gathers, made a body he knew and craved look like a perfectly formed marble sculpture. Her hair was a mass of glossy mahogany curls and waves, tumbling over her bare shoulders. Her makeup made her eyes look wide and clear, her cheeks sculpted and lips plump. It had taken everything in him to keep from pulling her into his arms and tasting them.

Hell, he'd been so mesmerized by Wynne, he'd forgotten all about Tabitha for a moment. It bothered him that Wynne still held such power over him, even now, after weeks of being apart. He'd had hundreds of submissives in his lifetime; none had taken such a firm hold of him before.

What was it about her? Was it her lovely eyes? Her luscious

mouth? That long, slender neck? Or perhaps it was something deeper. . . . ?

"Earth to Dierk." Tabitha snapped her fingers in front of his eyes. When he met her gaze, she asked, "Have a nice trip? Where'd you go?"

"I apologize. I'm . . . not myself tonight."

"Hmmmm." She twisted her mouth into a grimace. "I'm feeling a migraine coming on. They hit me out of the blue sometimes. I think I'd better call it a night."

"Do you need a ride home?"

"No, thank you. I'll get home just fine. I'll call for a car." She gave him a kiss on the cheek. "Thank you for a very nice evening. It was good meeting you."

"Yes, it was good meeting you, too."

Tabitha took a couple steps away, turned, smiled over her shoulder, said, "I think I'm going to have to cancel tomorrow night. I . . . hope you work it out with Wynne," and disappeared into the crowd, leaving him standing there, a glass of champagne in his hand.

Work what out with Wynne? There wasn't anything to work out. They'd scened once. That was all. He wasn't free to do anything else.

Even if he wanted to.

Shit, he had to get out of this town. Go far, far away.

Twilight was doing better, and he was hoping he could convince his brother Shadow it would run just fine without him. He had a life to get back to, one he'd once been perfectly content to live for the rest of his days.

Yes, he had a very nice life to get back to. Parties. Clubs. Dungeons.

He meandered through the crowd, lost in his thoughts. Until he saw her, standing in a corner, a glass of champagne lifted to her lips, a man he didn't know hovering over her like a hawk circling its prey.

She hadn't seen him yet. He had a chance to slip away unnoticed, to avoid what was sure to be another uncomfortable exchange.

He could turn around and walk away. He could.

No, he couldn't.

As if she sensed his gaze upon her, she looked his way and smiled. And just like that, something snapped and it was over. There was no way he could walk away from her now.

I shouldn't be doing this. I shouldn't be doing this.... His gaze never left her face as he wove his way through the throng, men knotted up in their best tuxedos, women in the latest couture, precious gems dripping from earlobes and necks and wrists. Delicious, sweet blood pulsing through their veins.

None of them mattered. Only Wynne.

The hawk spotted another sparrow and flew off.

"You lost someone." Wynne pointed at his empty arm, making him feel even shittier about their earlier conversation.

"Yeah, she had a headache. She decided to call it a night."

"Mmmm. That's too bad. I get headaches sometimes. They aren't fun."

He imagined her lying in bed, him sitting beside her, caressing her temples, rubbing her neck and shoulders. For some reason, he wanted more than her submission. He wanted to take care of her, to ease her pain when she was sick, to see love in her eyes when she lay beside him at night, to wipe her tears when she cried.

No, no, nonono.

Wynne emptied her glass in a series of quick gulps then set the empty champagne flute on a nearby table. Her gaze swept around the room. "Other than being ditched by your date, are you having a nice time?"

Her jealousy couldn't be clearer if she'd been wearing a neon sign on her chest.

"Tabitha wasn't my date," he blurted.

"Oh?" She flagged a waiter carrying a tray of glasses of champagne and snatched two. She went to work emptying the first right away.

"No, she was someone Rolf introduced me to."

Glass number one drained, Wynne set it down. "Well, I'd say from her boa constrictorlike grip on your arm she thought she was." She raised her glass. "This is great champagne. She might've gotten rid of that headache if she'd had a glass or two. Or three."

He gently removed the flute from Wynne's slightly unsteady grip. "I'm thinking you've had more than a glass or two, or three."

"Or five." She giggled, and oh shit did he like the way that sounded. Sweet and guileless, like the song of an angel. "I don't usually drink so much, but that champagne is really good. It's like drinking Kool-Aid."

"Where did Raven go?" He stole a glance around them.

"The little girls' room." Wynne's sweet face pulled into a pretty little scowl. "She's been gone a long time. Maybe I'd better go find her." She stumbled, the hem of her dress catching on the heel of her shoe. He caught her before she fell.

Damn, it felt good holding her. She sank into his arms, her body molding to his for at least a dozen heartbeats. His cock instantly sprang to a painful erection. A surge of sensual energy charged through his system.

They were magical, the two of them together. No way to deny it. He'd tried but he wouldn't any longer.

She tipped her head up, brushed aside a lock of hair that had fallen over her face, and smiled. "Thanks for saving me. This dress was made for an Amazon. Even with these ridiculous shoes, I'm too short." Bending over, while clinging to Dierk, she removed one shoe, then the other. "I'm okay now." She released him to gather the skirt in her fists, lifting it up to her knees. "Not the most dignified way to walk, but it's better than tripping and falling on my face."

"Yes, I suppose it is." He swallowed a chuckle. A sober Wynne was a delight. A drunk one, adorably vulnerable and honest.

"There she is." Wynne pointed over Dierk's shoulder. "I see Kristy." She waved a hand. "I don't think she sees me. This place is too fucking crowded."

Dierk twisted to look behind him. Raven was on the opposite side of the dungeon, standing in the center of a small gathering of people. He recognized them from Twilight, regulars, all of them. "We can head over there if you want. I'll help you."

"Thanks." She shoved her shoes into his hands then pranced ahead, proud as a queen on coronation day, and completely oblivious to the many curious stares she was gathering from onlookers. She stopped when she reached the group and dropped her skirt, much to Dierk's disappointment. She had very pretty calves, and he would never get tired of looking at them. "Hey Kristy, look who got ditched by his date."

Everyone stopped talking and looked at him.

He shrugged. "She wasn't my date."

They all gave him a yeah-sure-buddy smile.

Kristy turned to Wynne, who was swaying to music that nobody else could hear. "Wynnie, have you been drinking?"

She blinked a few times. They were very slow blinks. "I had a glass or two of champagne."

"Five," Dierk corrected, unable to hold back his chuckle this time.

Wynne gave him a squinty-eyed glare. "Tattletale. Now she's gonna tell me I have to go home."

Kristy laughed. "You're an adult. I'm not going to tell you you have to do anything."

"Well fine, then." After a beat, Wynne muttered, "I'm tired and my boobs are falling."

Kristy gave the people around her an apologetic smile. "I guess it's time to go."

Dierk stepped up to her and whispered, "I'd be happy to take her home, if you'd like to stay."

"You don't mind?" Raven looked more than grateful for the offer.

"Absolutely not. I was ready to go anyway. I promise I'll get her home safely."

"Oh hell, you know I trust you. Sure. That is, if Wynne is willing to go with you." She turned to Wynne. "Honey, Dierk's leaving now. He's offered to drive you home. Is that okay?"

Wynne scrutinized him. "Okayyyy. I guess I'll go with Dierk, since he insists." She leaned over and said, "Probably doesn't want to be seen leaving by himself."

Kristy laughed. "Yeah, that's gotta be it."

16

"So sorry your new plaything got a headache tonight," Wynne said as she settled into Dierk's zoomy little sports car. The vehicle was sleek and sexy, and it still smelled really good, just like its owner.

Too bad the owner was such an ass.

"Yes, thanks. You've already . . . never mind."

"I've already what?" Feeling a little too warm, she fiddled with the window controls until she had her window open just enough, not so wide that a cyclone blew through the car, and not too little. The fresh air felt good and it seemed to be helping her clear her head, a good thing. She was pretty effed up. She couldn't remember the last time she'd had so much to drink. It didn't help that she was a lightweight when it came to alcohol. "Please tell me I didn't make an idiot of myself tonight."

"No, you didn't."

"Good. Because I never drink this much."

"I suspected as much."

She couldn't help laughing. "Is it that obvious?"

"No." He was lying, but that was okay. He was doing it so

she wouldn't feel so stupid. What a sweet man. An asshole for rejecting her, but sweet, too.

She wanted to kiss him. She decided that was a damn fine idea. When the car stopped at a traffic light, she unfastened her seat belt and leaned toward him.

"Where are you going?" he asked.

"Nowhere." She pressed her lips to his cheek. It wasn't the kind of kiss she would have liked to give him, but since the light would change any second anyway, it would have to be enough. "I just wanted to do that." As she settled back in her seat and refastened her seat belt, she noticed his face and neck were red. "Did I embarrass you?"

"No, not at all." He turned on the air conditioning. She guessed he was warm, too. That was probably why his face was red. How silly to think her kiss had embarrassed him. Why should he be embarrassed? They were alone.

She laughed at herself. "Yeah, that was a stupid thing to ask."

He smiled and cheerful little crinkles creased out from the corners of his eyes. They were so cute, and how she adored the way his face changed when he smiled. It came alive. "You don't do or say anything stupid."

"How kind of you to say so."

The car stopped. Had to be another traffic light.

No, he was shifting the car into park.

She looked out the window. *Home? Already? Damn.* "Well that was a quick trip. Thanks for the ride. With things being so awkward between us in the past, it was really nice of you to offer." She reached for the door.

"No, let me get it."

Such the gentleman.

He exited the vehicle, walked around and opened her door for her. And, as she hoped, he gave her a hand getting out of the car. The damn thing sat so low, it was like sitting on the ground.

She leaned a little on him as she walked to her building, down the main hallway, and up to her apartment door.

She fished in her purse for her keys.

She dug deeper.

They weren't in there.

"Oh shit," she muttered.

"What's wrong?"

"I didn't bring my keys. I didn't think I'd need them. Kristy drove."

"Oh."

"Kristy knew I didn't have . . . oh, that sneaky little bitch." She grimaced. "I'm sorry but I think we both got caught in one of Kristy's little traps." She tried the door, even though she knew for a fact that they'd locked it when they left earlier. "Maybe you can get one of the windows—"

"That's okay. I'll take you back to my place. You can sleep there."

Wynne sighed. Her head fell forward, her forehead thunking against the locked door. "I'm so sorry. My friend is going to pay for this."

Dierk gently lifted her chin, coaxing her to look at him. "Don't worry about it. I have a spare room. I'll bring you back in the morning."

"Okay, then. I suppose I have no choice, unless I want to sit out here in the hall until Kristy decides to come home. And knowing her that'll be tomorrow sometime."

"Let's go." Patiently, he led her back to his car, helped her get situated in the seat, then ran around to his side and got in. They were both quiet as he drove what turned out to be about ten miles or so to a nice condominium complex close to Twilight. His condo was of the two-storied variety. Detached. Brown brick. With a big garage door, front and center. He hit the remote as they pulled up the driveway and the door lifted, allowing him to pull the car inside. "Here we are." He cut off the engine and hit the button to shut the door, closing them in the garage.

Like most garages, his smelled like gasoline and car exhaust. But it was absolutely spotless, not a hammer or lawn mower or weed whacker in sight.

He ushered her through an interior door, leading into a narrow hallway off the kitchen. The floors were all gleaming wood. The walls, she realized as she followed him around the bend and up the stairs, were all painted a warm taupe color. And the rooms were all furnished, but sparsely. She couldn't say why, but it was missing something. It didn't look lived in.

"This is a nice place," she said.

"Thanks." He stepped into a good-sized bedroom. "Here you go. You have your own bath over here." He opened a door on the opposite side of the room. "I'll get you something to sleep in."

"Oh, that's okay. I don't sleep in clothes."

He visibly swallowed and the red returned to his face and neck. It was a nice shade, complemented his eyes.

She couldn't help grinning. "Is something wrong?"

"Not at all. I'll be in the room at the opposite end of the hall. Let me know if you need anything." He hesitated, and, her courage fortified by the ample supply of alcohol streaming through her veins, she flattened her body against his and wrapped her arms around her neck.

Ahhh, now that felt good and right. She pressed her ear to his chest. Her entire body thrummed to the steady thump-wump that beat against his rib cage.

He didn't exactly hug her back at first, which made for a somewhat awkward moment. But a few seconds later, he lifted his arms and wrapped them around her. He even cradled the back of her head in a hand. Oh yes, that was so much better.

She closed her eyes and soaked in all the yummy Dierk loving. His fingers massaged her scalp. His other hand was lower, flattened against the small of her back, and the skin beneath it tingled like it had never tingled before. A steady drumbeat kicked up between her legs. She smooshed herself tighter against him.

There was quite a hard bulge pressed against her, right about her tummy level. Just because she was feeling naughty, she started moving against him. In exchange, he curled his fingers in her hair and pulled, easing her head back.

Their eyes met. His were very dark, his expression a mask of hard male need. She shuddered, literally.

"I'm sorry," he muttered. Slowly, he released her, but that didn't keep her from feeling like she was going to fall over. He had it all wrong. He wasn't supposed to leave her now, he was supposed to kiss her until she couldn't stand, and then he was supposed to carry her over to that nice, big bed and fuck her until she was in heaven. "I shouldn't—"

She nodded. "Oh yes, you should."

"No." He headed for the door, this time looking extremely sure of himself.

"Why?" She didn't follow him, although she wanted to. "I like you. You seem to like me, if that lump in your pants is any indicator. So why do you keep pushing me away?"

"Because it's best."

Her insides were twisting and turning, tying themselves into knots. And acid was burning through her veins. This time she couldn't stop herself from going to him. She needed to be close so she could look into those dark eyes of his and see if she could figure out the truth. "Best for whom?"

He visibly inhaled, exhaled. "You."

"If you think you know what's good for me, you're wrong. You don't have a clue."

"Don't I?" Suddenly, he grabbed her upper arms and hauled her against him. He looked down upon her face with open passion and longing, and she was captivated, ensnared by the emotion she read in his eyes. He tipped his head, and, expecting a kiss at last, she closed her eyes and held her breath.

She waited.

Waited.

"I told you that first day," he practically growled. "We can't do this. It goes against everything I believe in."

She opened her eyes to glare at him. "I don't get you. You don't believe in caring about people? Expressing your feelings? Giving pleasure? I guess I don't know how to play by your rules, Master. I make a very poor slave. But I can't deny my heart its deepest wanting."

"Then you force me to." He released her, and she practically crumpled to the floor. "I will be leaving soon, returning to the life I left behind. You can't go with me."

"Why not? Give me a reason that makes sense and I won't ever bother you again."

He scrubbed his face with his hands. "I'm not the man you think you know."

"Yeah, I'm beginning to see that. You're not brave and powerful and honorable." Her eyes and nose were burning, but she refused to let herself cry. "You're a bastard."

"Yes, I'm a bastard. And worse." He started to say something more but stopped. Instead, he turned and headed for the door.

"Maybe someday you'll stop running," she yelled after him.

He left the room without saying another word, closing the door behind him.

Devastated and furious, she kicked off her shoes and stripped out of the dress. She tried lying down, but, even though she was still pretty buzzed, she couldn't fall asleep. She opted to take a hot bath, hoping the warm water would help her relax.

Really, she knew there was basically no chance she'd sleep

tonight. Not with so much going through her head. But she went through the motions anyway. She filled the tub and soaked. And soaked, and soaked and soaked. Until the skin on her hands and feet was shriveled up like a prune. Still, when she stepped out of the tub, she felt no more ready for sleep than she had been before she'd started.

It was useless.

She checked the closet, hoping to find something to wear, but she found it empty. She searched the dressers. Again, empty. This place, as pretty as it was, had no life. It felt like a model home that had been staged, or, like a movie set, designed to make people believe it was lived in when actually it was lifeless.

With no other option but to put on that dress—out of the question—she fashioned a toga out of the flat sheet and headed downstairs. There wouldn't be much on TV at this hour, but she hoped she'd find something distracting, maybe a movie on LMN. Those were always good for reminding her how good she had it. Nobody was trying to kill her, she didn't have psycho family members destroying her life, and she hadn't been kidnapped and sold into slavery.

She turned on the television—a puny set by today's standards—and made herself comfy on the couch, the remote in her fist. She clicked a few times and quickly realized Dierk didn't have cable.

Infomercial.

Infomercial.

And infomercial. Blech.

Something rustled by the hallway. Instinctively, she leaned over to look.

Dierk. In a snug tank shirt and a pair of shorts. He looked amazing. Her heart twisted.

This sucked.

She cut off the TV and set the remote on the coffee table, where she had found it. "Sorry, did the television wake you? There's nothing on so I'm heading back up to bed."

"No, I wasn't asleep. I don't sleep well at night." He crossed his arms over his chest, displaying a don't-get-too-close vibe she couldn't misread, no matter how much alcohol was clouding her vision.

"Usually I sleep okay." She bit her lip to keep from saying more. There was no point; he'd made that clear.

He tipped his head. "Nice outfit."

"Yeah, well, I didn't want to wake you, but since you're already awake, do you mind finding me something comfortable to wear? I guess I should've accepted the offer when you made it."

"Not a problem. I have plenty of T-shirts. . . ." He led her back up the stairs and down the hall. At the door to his room, she hesitated, hanging back in the hallway. But from her vantage point, she was able to watch him well enough. This was the most undressed she'd seen the man, and wow, did he have a body. She'd felt those muscles under his clothes plenty of times, but to see them flex as he moved, it was enough to make her warm and tingly all over.

She watched as he bent over to get something from his bottom drawer. Nice ass. She watched as he reached high in his closet to get something from the top shelf. Oh, those shoulders. And she watched as he strolled toward her.

It just wasn't right that he should be that perfect and yet so unreachable.

When he handed her the clothes, their gazes locked, their fingers brushed against each other, and a huge jolt of sensual energy shot between them. It was almost enough to take her breath away.

He couldn't tell her he didn't feel it, too. That connection. That magic. She could read it on his face, see it in every plane and bulge on his tense body. That only infuriated her more.

What could be so wrong with him or his life that he couldn't follow his heart's desire?

"Dierk—"

"Please." He stepped backward. "I don't want to regret anything I say or do tonight."

Her eyes were burning again, dammit. She hated this man for making her feel this way. But on the other hand, she adored him for it, too. Until now, she hadn't realized what true wanting was, what genuine passion felt like. It was absolute hell. And heaven. Bliss. And misery. If she'd married John, she never would have experienced anything even remotely close to it.

"I wish I could understand," she said on a sigh, backing into the hallway. "And, more than anything, I wish I could tell my heart to stop aching for you." She turned to head back to her room, but he caught her wrist and jerked her back around.

One instant she was standing in the hallway, Dierk's clothes folded in her arms, and the next she was flattened against the wall, Dierk's hot body blocking her escape, not that she wanted to go anywhere. She couldn't tip her head back to look into his eyes, not with the wall there, but she couldn't care less. He was close, touching her, his fingers digging in her hair, his knee pushing between her thighs. "Dammit, Wynne. Holy Hell," he repeated over and over.

She was on fire. Her pussy burned for his touch, and she couldn't help rocking her hips back and forth, grinding against his leg. The friction only made it worse.

Would he kiss her? Would he fuck her with his cock, not his fingers, not a toy, but that glorious rod? She'd waited so long, dreamed, wished, hoped.

He was trembling against her, his skin searing to the touch but smooth as satin. She stroked his arms, her fingertips mapping the crests between thick muscles and blood vessels beating with life.

He backed up a little and she thought the moment was over.

She felt herself slumping forward, having lost his support, but he caught her, scooped her off her feet, and carried her down to her room.

Could it be? Had he decided . . . ?

He set her on the bed and stared down at her with a fierce, dark expression that made her want to whimper. Then he bent down and kissed her and she really did whimper. More than once.

His kiss was soft at first, a reluctant, patient taste. Oh so good. Oh so devastating, as she'd expected it would be.

He didn't have to use his tongue to make her surrender. His lips were all he needed. She was his to do with as he wished. Body, mind, and soul.

His hands held her shoulders, pressing them down into the mattress while his mouth took her captive. She never wanted it to end, this sweet torment. This was the moment she'd craved, and it was more magical than she could have imagined.

And then he deepened the kiss and she lost all ability to think. His tongue slipped into her mouth and she was at his mercy, powerless to do anything but give everything he asked of her.

This was where she wanted to be: with Dierk, beneath him, giving everything she had and was to him. She hoped, as she poured out her emotions in her kiss, that he wouldn't run away again.

His hand found an opening in her toga, and soon his fingertip was tracing a line down the center of her torso. Between her breasts, down her stomach, to her shaved mound. She tried to part her legs, but he crawled overtop of her and caught them between his knees. Damn him.

Within moments, she was tight all over and trembling, a hard, steady beat pulsing between her legs, her head spinning, her breath coming in hard little gasps. Still, he kissed her. Still, he teased her with soft touches and strokes.

"Promise me you won't stop," she whispered against his mouth. "Promise me you won't let me go again."

"I . . . can't promise." He sat back and gazed down upon her. He looked at her lovingly but his eyes were still dark and full of emotion. "You don't know me. You have no idea who I really am."

"But that's only because you haven't let me know you. You hide yourself in shadows. Why?"

"Because I'm not free to give myself to anyone."

"Are you saying . . . you're married?"

He looked away. "No, not yet."

Her blood chilled. She curled her fingers into tight fists. The air in the room thinned. She couldn't breathe. "What does that mean?"

"It means I'm engaged."

Certain now that she would cry, she grabbed two corners of the sheet and pulled them around herself, encasing her body and arms. She swallowed a sob. "Well, I guess that explains a lot."

"I do care about you. You know that. But I have promised . . . I can't back out now." Ironically, he backed away from her, moving off the bed. He rubbed his kiss-swollen mouth with his hand.

"I see." She was going to be sick. Her insides felt like they'd been slashed through with a knife. "I've never seen you with . . . her. Oh wait. Please tell me it isn't Tabitha."

"It isn't Tabitha. She was interested in becoming a member of Twilight."

"Oh, I think she was interested in more than that," she snapped, letting her anger slip through in the sarcastic comment.

"I had a suspicion. My brother set her up for disappointment. He doesn't approve of my . . ." He took yet another step backward. Another, and another. At the door, he paused. "I wish I'd known."

"Known what?"

He didn't answer right away. "How it felt to be with you."

"I guess I'm sorry for you then."

His expression hardened. "I'd rather have your rage than your pity. That's why I couldn't tell you before now."

She dragged her hands over her eyes. "Sorry. But that's all you'll get from me."

17

"He's what!" Kristy screeched. She clapped her hands over her ears and moaned. "It's too early for this kind of shock. I need caffeine. Lots of it, and then you're going to tell me what happened last night." Barefoot and wearing a pair of cropped sweats and a Duran Duran T-shirt, Kristy shuffled into the kitchen.

Following her, with the intention of getting a big glass of water and some aspirin for her hangover, Wynne muttered, "I never would've guessed."

"Me neither. If I had, I wouldn't have encouraged you to go after him."

"I know."

"I asked around, but nobody knew much about him, outside of his relationship to Rolf." After filling the coffeemaker and switching it on, Kristy gave her a long hug. "I'm so sorry. Engaged? The bastard."

"But that's just it. He isn't a bastard. He didn't do anything to encourage my feelings. Exactly the opposite, he kept discouraging me. Right from the beginning, he's been avoiding me. Until last night . . ." Wynne sat at the kitchen table, plunked her elbows on the tabletop, and dropped her chin on her fists.

"What happened?" Kristy looked so miserable, it made Wynne feel worse.

"Um . . . nothing," she lied. She just couldn't tell Kristy everything, knowing it would make her friend pity her more. "He took me to his house and let me sleep in his spare bedroom. I was wasted, and I was an idiot, but he didn't try to take advantage of the situation. Not once." She sighed. "I think it's time to adopt some cats and retire from the dating scene."

"Oh, honey . . ." Kristy, a full cup of coffee in her hand, sat beside her. "Maybe a trip to Twilight'll make things better?"

"I don't know." Wynne shook two aspirin out of the bottle. She raised her glass. "I gave in and made an appointment with Rolf for tomorrow night, but I think I'm going to cancel it."

Kristy lifted her coffee cup. "Fair enough. I won't try to change your mind if that's what you want to do." She tapped her cup against Wynne's. "To mending hearts."

"I'll drink to that."

That bastard was meeting someone today, and Dierk was pretty damn sure he knew who that someone was. This was why he'd punched the hole in the wall. This was also why he'd decided it was better if he stayed locked in his office with the monitors shut off.

If he saw them together, he would have no choice but to do something about it.

His plan would have worked if only he'd been able to avoid leaving his office. But fate, being the bitch she was, had thrown a wrench in his plans. He'd had to go out into the main dungeon and he'd seen them.

One minute, he was standing a safe distance away, discussing a problem with his security manager and the other, he was in an up close and personal staredown with Rolf. There was no way in hell he was going to lose.

Wynne looked annoyed, or maybe angry. She had every right to be. So did his fucking brother, but he couldn't help himself. She was his, dammit. His. No other man could adore her as much as he did. Worship her. Love her.

He ached to tell her. At least then she'd know. But he couldn't, dammit. It would hurt her too much.

"What are you doing, brother?" Rolf said through gritted teeth. His eyes narrowed into a hard glare. "I am a member in good standing and have broken no rules."

"I know," Dierk snapped.

"Dierk, Rolf?" Wynne set one hand on each of their shoulders.

How he hated her touching any man but him. The sight made his insides coil into hard knots. Practically trembling from the effort of holding in his building rage, he cupped her cheek and stared into her lovely eyes. "Wynne, it's okay. I need to talk to my brother for a minute. Only a minute."

Rolf gave her an assenting nod.

She stepped back and wrapped her arms around herself. "O-okay. I'll go get a drink at the bar—"

"Anything you want. It's on the house." Dierk jerked his head toward the door.

Rolf followed him back into his office but, even after a succinct and no doubt less than friendly invitation to sit, he stood just inside the door. "We're alone now. So what's this all about?"

"Wynne."

"Yeah, I kinda guessed that much." Rolf leaned a hip against a chair. "What about her?"

"You can't play with her anymore."

"What gives you the right to tell me that?"

"I love her."

* * *

Rolf shook his head. He didn't just hear what he thought he had. No way in hell.

His brother Dierk didn't fall in love with women, he used them and then disposed of them when he was through. The word *love* didn't exist in his vocabulary. How many times had Dierk told him that love wasn't real? That it was a myth, like the legend of the magical unicorn? A pretty figment of humanity's collective imagination.

He looked deeper into his brother's eyes and echoed, "You *love* her?"

Dierk jerked his hand through his hair and dropped his gaze. A heavy silence fell between them for a few strained seconds, which was finally broken by Dierk's confession. "Yes, I love her. I love her so much it's making me crazy. I don't just want her, I need her. I don't just want to see her, I live to see her. I don't just long for her, I ache for her. I hurt when she is away from me. I think about nobody but her. I dream about no one but her. I am hers."

Now Rolf could remain on his feet no longer. He didn't merely sit, he practically collapsed into the chair. His brother's words struck him like a physical blow and they hurt like hell.

He'd come to care for Wynne, too. Still, he couldn't deny one fact. He didn't love her like Dierk did.

Dierk curled his fingers, fisting his hair, the heels of his hands pressed into his eye sockets. "I can't stand this. I can't face another minute without her."

"If you could, would you marry her?"

"Oh hell, if I could, I would Join with her, but I know neither can be. Only the king can Join with his bride. And I am engaged to another woman."

"You would *Join* with her?" Rolf repeated.

"If it were possible."

"Well hell. You must really love her, then." Rolf patted his brother on the shoulder and headed for the door. "I have a few errands to run. It seems you have a problem, Dierk. A big one." He paused at the door. "But I'll say this: Wynne could have no better man love her, my brother, and you know you could have no better woman love you."

Something flared in Dierk's eyes. "Do you think she loves me?"

"You'll have to find that out for yourself. You have my word, I won't stand in your way."

Rolf left, hoping his brother would find a way to take hold of the happiness that was within his grasp.

It seemed Wynne wasn't the only woman who had decided to complicate things for him.

Dierk was beginning to believe all women were prone to such whims. Either that, or he had the worst luck in the world to have found two such women.

His fiancée had learned where he was staying and had decided to join him. In a normal relationship, that wouldn't have been a problem. In fact, it would have more likely been welcome. But in his case, it was far from welcome.

It wasn't that he didn't love Olivia. She was, by most men's standards, everything one would want in a wife. The problem was Dierk didn't want a wife. Or rather, he hadn't wanted a wife when he'd made his promise to her. That was done out of duty.

Now, he found he did want a wife—but not Olivia. However, bound by duty and honor, he couldn't break off the engagement.

He had a wife he didn't want.

He had broken Wynne's heart.

His own heart was breaking.

He was in hell and he had nobody to blame but himself.

He heard a car outside. The engine cut off. A door slammed. She was here. He hadn't seen her since the last time he'd asked for her hand.

If only he could live a certain night over again. He would gladly pay any price.

But nothing, no amount of money or property, would allow him to turn back time.

The doorbell rang. He hadn't expected her to ring the door. After all, he'd told her this would be her home as long as they remained in the area. He went to answer it and found her looking cheerful and pretty, as he remembered her.

"Hello, Dierk." Olivia smiled as she stepped into her temporary home. She glanced around and he watched her, catching a hint of disappointment. "This is . . . quaint."

"I warned you it wasn't what you left behind."

"That's okay. I'd rather be in a log cottage with you than in that giant cave by myself." She set her handbag on the console table. "Will you give me the grand tour?"

"I'd be happy to."

"Thank you." She took his arm as he led her through the small condo, pointing out the things he thought would interest her most. When it was time to show her the guestroom, which would be her room, he felt himself stiffen. The memories of last week were still fresh in his mind, the vision of Wynne lying on the bed, her hair fanned out over the pillow, the sheet parted, revealing a tempting slice of ivory skin. . . .

"Dierk, it's a good thing I came. It looks like this place could use a woman's touch."

"Yes, I'm sure it could."

What price he would pay for one mistake.

It had been two months since Wynne had spent the night at Dierk's house and still her heart did a little somersault every time the phone rang, someone knocked on the door, or she saw a black sports car. If she thought it had been hard getting over John, she had no idea what she was in for. That was a walk in the park compared to this.

Now, as she rushed to answer the knock at the door, her heart was in her throat and an irrational expectation was making it beat so hard and fast that she felt a little faint. There was absolutely no reason to think it was Dierk, and still she hoped.

"Hello, Wynne," Rolf greeted, a huge red gift bag in his arms.

"Hi. What a surprise." She stepped aside and welcomed him in with a sweep of the arm. "Come in."

"I hope you don't mind. I saw this and I thought of you. It's your birthday today, isn't it?"

"That's very sweet of you to remember. Thanks."

"You'd better wait until you see what it is before you call me sweet." He winked.

She chuckled. "Let's see what it is, then."

It really was too bad that she didn't have the same feelings for Rolf as she did for Dierk. He was just as good looking as his brother, maybe a little better. And he was patient, kind, and thoughtful, too. If he wanted to be married, she hoped he would find the right girl soon.

If only she felt for him what she did for Dierk.

She accepted the bag from Rolf and set it on the coffee table. Inside, she found a stripper pole kit, and instantly she doubled over with laughter. "Ohmygod, you're ridiculous. Where did you find this?"

"Where anyone finds the most obscure, out-of-the-ordinary things: eBay, of course."

"Well, thank you. I think. I can't say for sure whether I'll install it."

A tense silence fell between them.

He cleared his throat. "Wynne, I know my brother hurt you, and I'm sorry. I honestly thought, after seeing you two together, that he'd break his engagement with Olivia." Rolf shoved his fingers through his hair. "He doesn't deserve you."

"Hey, it's my fault I got hurt, so don't put the blame where it shouldn't lay. He was honest and told me there couldn't be any emotional entanglements. I was stupid and decided to start tying the knots."

"I still don't agree with what he did. Maybe some women can handle a situation like that, but you . . ." He looked away, shifted his weight from one foot to the other. "You're different." When his gaze returned to her face, it was full of emotion, the kind she'd longed to see in Dierk's eyes.

Her heart slid to her toes.

Now she knew what it felt like to have unwanted affection directed her way. Talk about a turning of the tables.

A heavy sense of responsibility fell on her shoulders. Had she somehow encouraged this?

"I'll take that as a compliment." She chewed on her lip, uncertain what to say next. She could read in Rolf's body language that he was a little nervous. He stood sort of stiffly, like his arms and legs couldn't bend. "Rolf, you fault your brother, and so I feel I need to be very honest with you. I like you, very much. I care about you. And I appreciate how kind and patient and supportive you've been since the very first day we met. But there's something missing between us, and I don't want you to be misled and think we might . . . things might go a certain way between us. It simply can't. Even if your brother does marry someone else."

"Sure." He smiled, but the expression didn't reach his eyes. "I just thought . . . fuck, I don't know what I thought." A wry smile on his face, he shook his head and started toward the door.

Wynne, feeling like shit, touched his arm. "Rolf. I wish things were different, that my feelings for Dierk would evaporate and I could fall in love with you. Because you are a good man. But that's why I can't lead you on, because you're a good man and you deserve a woman who is so in love with you, she can't live a minute without you."

"Yeah." He stepped through the door. "Happy birthday, Wynne. I hope all your wishes come true."

"Thanks." She started to close the door, but hesitated when he lifted his hand to stop her.

He said, "I don't know if this'll make it better for you or worse, but he doesn't love her. He never has. And as far as I can see, she doesn't love him either. But he's too damn stubborn to break the engagement."

"I don't understand. If they don't love each other, why are they getting married?"

"It's a long story."

"I've got all night." She grabbed his hand and tugged, practically dragging him back into the apartment. "Please, tell me."

"I will if you promise me one thing."

"Anything."

"Give me your word you won't let him hurt you anymore. No matter what happens."

No matter what? "You have my word." She shook his hand, sealing the deal.

18

Dierk looked at the clock for the tenth time in the last hour. It seemed like every morning Olivia was returning home later and later, yesterday barely making it back before sunrise.

He was not jealous. He was not angry. But he was a little worried. With his venom pumping through her veins, exposure to sunlight would cost her a great price. She wouldn't be destroyed like he would, but she would suffer some side effects, none of them pleasant.

The lock rattled. The doorknob twisted.

He could go to bed now. She was home. He started for the stairs. She looked rumpled, a satisfied smile lighting her face.

She was freshly fucked.

Saying nothing, he turned and continued up the stairs.

He supposed she was disappointed in his reaction, or rather, his lack of a reaction. Even though she didn't love him, he knew she still wished to know he noticed and cared about her on some level.

He did. Just not on the level he would if she were another woman. A very special woman.

Still, this new arrangement they had agreed upon, which was only a slight adjustment to the first—a fact for which he was grateful—would suit them both. They would live together from this point on, but even after they married, they would not share a bed. She could fuck any man she liked. And Dierk would take any submissive he liked. There would be, however, and could be no lovers, no affairs that involved emotional commitments or feelings. That was the line they agreed would not be crossed.

On the surface, it seemed fair enough. They each had satisfied their obligation to one another. In time, he expected it would be good enough.

Olivia followed him, pausing at her bedroom door.

He glanced back at her.

As usual, her hair was a mass of tangled waves, and her makeup, usually perfect, was smudged around her mouth and eyes. Her clothes were hanging from her body but they weren't fastened, revealing slivers of skin and black lacy underclothes beneath.

To the average man, he supposed she looked sexy, with those kiss-swollen lips and come-hither eyes. But to him, she looked used and tired and a little sad, and he realized then that maybe this arrangement wasn't enough for her either, that fulfilling an obligation was worse than the consequences of failing.

"Hello, sweetheart," she slurred. "Still awake, I see."

"I am. Would you like a drink before retiring?"

"Sure, why not?"

They headed back downstairs together. She accepted a glass of Guignolet, a cherry liqueur she developed a taste for while living in France, and sat on the couch. He poured himself a scotch and sat across from her, in an armchair.

She took a sip from her glass and set it down. "Do you suppose we've delayed the inevitable long enough?"

"It seems," he agreed, fully aware of where this conversation was leading. There couldn't be another reason for her coming to him now.

"Every year, you propose we get married, and every year, I ask you to give me more time." She leaned back, curled the fingers of her right hand over the arm of the couch. "This year I will not ask you that."

"Then you're ready to set a date for our wedding?"

"Oh, I didn't say that." Olivia stood, and confused, he watched as she finished the rest of her glass then walked to the bar to refill it. Once she returned to her seat, she continued, "It has been a very long time since you met me and so much has changed. Thanks to you, I'm not the frightened, destitute young girl I once was. I've gained wealth, power, and a great deal of wisdom since then. Who wouldn't, after living for over two hundred years?" She chuckled, emptied her glass for the second time, and set it on the table. "You proposed out of a sense of duty, and I respect you for it, and for the many kindnesses you've shown me all this time, but I am ready now to reclaim my mortality and make my own choices." She stood again, nodded. "There, I've said it, and I feel so much better. I didn't think I would ever find the courage."

Shocked, he immediately rose to his feet. He didn't dare believe he was free. It would be too wonderful. "Olivia, are you sure? I won't turn my back on you if you need my support, and the thought of your growing old—"

Olivia pressed her hand to his mouth. "Please, Dierk. Your venom has allowed me to outlive my sisters' children, their children, and the children of their children. I've watched everyone around me grow from mewling infants to frail old men and women. And I've waited all that time for the one thing you have denied me: your love."

"Olivia—"

"No. Don't say it." She turned from him. "I know you love me, as a brother does a sister." When she faced him again, her lip was quivering, her hands trembling. "But that wasn't what I wanted, what I craved." She took his hand in hers. "Try to understand. I want true passion, a love that cannot be suppressed for fear it might destroy me if I hold it back. That kind of love I will never share with you, especially now that I've seen you feel it for another."

"Seen? You couldn't have seen anything, because I have done—"

"Please, Dierk." She released his hand. "This is the time for truths. Don't lie to yourself now."

He stared into her eyes. They were dear eyes, and he saw so much in them. Respect. Appreciation. Gratitude. And encouragement. They belonged to a very dear and trusted friend and a woman who had once needed him so desperately, she'd been happy to accept a loveless match. But that wasn't the case any longer.

Ironically, he wasn't happy to accept a loveless match anymore either. Because, as Olivia had said, he had given himself to someone. He did share a love like she had described—how had she put it? A love that couldn't be suppressed.

She pulled his engagement ring off her slender finger. "Don't worry about me. I have everything I will need to live the rest of my days comfortably, thanks to your generosity. And I still have a young face and body and an irrational hope that I might find what you have." She handed him the ring.

He gazed down at it, still unsure whether he could believe this was happening. When he'd made his promise to Olivia's father—to support his daughter, to provide for her, and to eventually wed her on the day she agreed to marry him—the colonies were fighting for independence from the king. That was a long time ago.

Since then, the world had changed drastically, but he continued to keep his promise. He kept her comfortable, provided her with a handsome income, as many houses as she cared to own, along with all the servants she would need to run them, and jewelry, furs, gowns, everything she desired.

Never had he expected the onetime penniless youngest daughter of a bankrupt baronet to one day decide to walk away from it all.

"Will you write to me?" he asked.

She smiled and nodded. "I will, if you like." She hugged him, and he held her for the last time, loving her more than he ever had, for giving him the most precious gift anyone had ever given him. His freedom. "Good-bye, my dear Dierk. And thank you."

He managed a final thank-you as she stood at the front door and waved good-bye.

"So, tell me." Wynne was sitting on the edge of her seat, literally, waiting for Rolf to explain why Dierk was engaged to a woman he didn't love. Who did such a thing these days, who agreed to marry someone out of duty? "Why is Dierk engaged if he doesn't love this woman?"

"Because he promised her father he would marry her."

"Okay." She sat back. "So that's it? He promised and so it's done. I thought you said it was a long story?"

He chuckled. "I did. I'm just getting started."

"Ah. Okay." She positioned a throw pillow on the couch, and settled in nice and comfy, ready to hear the whole story. "Spill it. I'm ready."

"Let me see. It's been a long time since I told this story to anyone. . . ." Rolf grinned when she shot him a warning glare. "Impatient?"

"Naw."

"Her father was a baronet."

"Baronet?" she echoed.

"It's a title of honor, given by the king of England."

"You mean queen? England has a queen," she corrected.

"Or queen." He cleared his throat. "Anyway, her father suffered a run of bad luck and found himself in debt, but he found his daughter a profitable match—"

"Profitable match, like a business partner?" she asked, somewhat confused.

Rolf cleared his throat again. His eyes twinkled. "Not exactly."

"I don't get it." She studied his face. He was looking all too cheerful for it to mean something dreadful, but still a very disturbing possibility kept creeping into her thoughts. "Tell me he did not literally sell his daughter to pay his debt."

"He did, in a way."

"That's outrageous! I can't believe anyone would do such a thing. Was she a child?"

"No, she wasn't a child."

"Well thank God for that." She actually felt herself exhale with relief. "I suppose many shocking things are done behind closed doors. I've . . . watched a few Lifetime movies to have some notion." At Rolf's shrug, she asked, "So, Dierk agreed to accept this baronet's daughter as payment for some kind of debt he was owed?"

"No. He wasn't owed any money and wasn't part of the original agreement. Another man was. But one night there was a misunderstanding, and that quarrel led to a fight, and Olivia's intended was killed. Dierk didn't mean to kill him—"

She felt herself gaping. "Dierk . . . *killed* a man?"

Rolf's expression turned grim. "It was an accident, one my brother has paid for dearly. Once he heard about the baronet's daughter, he felt obligated to provide what he had taken from her family. Thus, he agreed to take the other man's place and take her as his bride. But Olivia, being a woman with romantic notions, told him she would remain his fiancée until the day she had decided upon a date. I think she has been waiting for some sign from Dierk, a sign he hasn't given yet. It's been many years, and still he waits for her to tell him when they will be married."

After a pause, she asked, "And that's the full story?"

"It is."

"Wow." She stared down at her hands, not for any reason, other than to be looking at something inconsequential so she could concentrate on absorbing the details of what she'd just been told.

It was a sad, tragic tale, one that would have easily been extracted from a book or movie. And one that seemed so out of place in the world she lived in, where debts were paid with credit cards or taken into bankruptcy court, not paid by handing off one's offspring. But she supposed, having lived a somewhat sheltered life, anything was possible in certain parts of the globe. She knew so little about the world outside of the lower-middle-class American Midwest life she'd been born into. Both Dierk and Rolf spoke with a slight accent. It was possible—no, likely—they'd lived in a foreign land where things were very different from Michigan.

"He won't break the engagement because he feels indebted to the baronet," Rolf added.

"I understand now." Not sure how she felt, she lifted her gaze to Rolf. In some ways, what he'd told her gave her more appreciation and respect for Dierk. To step into another man's place and take a wife he did not love, out of a sense of duty, was remarkable. And to take a commitment seriously, even though his fiancée had put him off for years, was even more extraordinary. Yes, he scened with women in dungeons. He'd scened with her, and she knew she wasn't the first or the last. And he had almost lost control that one time in his house, but never had he made love to her.

As far as she could tell, he had remained faithful to his fiancée since she'd met him.

She could just imagine what kind of self-control and dedication staying true to such a commitment had taken, especially if he'd been waiting years and years for his fiancée to agree to marry him.

Rolf glanced at the clock and stood. "I should get going. It's getting late."

She hopped to her feet. "Okay." She grabbed his hand and gave it a little squeeze. "Thank you for telling me about Dierk. I'm not sure how I feel about everything, but I think it helped."

"You're welcome." He slipped out the door, but before he walked away, he gave her one last doleful look over his shoulder. "Good-bye, Wynne."

19

Wynne slowly strolled down the aisle, her gaze hopping from one book cover to another. In the paranormal romance section now, she wasn't finding anything new or interesting. Vampires. More vampires. Bleh. There was a werewolf. Another. Yawn.

She wanted something new, fresh, a story about some foreign mythos she'd never heard of, an obscure but really interesting legend or a unique take on something that'd already been done to death.

She checked her cell phone. It was almost seven. The store was closing in about ten minutes, and Rolf would be here any minute. They had made plans to check out the pub a couple doors down. It wasn't a date-date, just a meet-a-friend-for-drinks thing. Kristy was supposed to meet up with them a little later, after she finished up at Twilight.

Out of desperation, Wynne picked up a vampire novel that looked semi-interesting. The little bell hanging above the door clanked, signaling the arrival of a customer, maybe Rolf. She turned, stepping out from behind a tall wall of shelves, and checked the door.

That wasn't Rolf.

Her heart did a somersault. She turned right around and practically dove behind the bookcase again, hoping Dierk hadn't seen her. She didn't want to talk to him. She didn't want to hear his voice. She didn't want to look into those dark eyes.

"Hiding?" he said, his voice light with laugher.

She kept her gaze lowered, knowing if he was smiling, she would be enthralled, and then she'd make an idiot of herself. "No way. I dropped my book. Gotta go." She took a step in the opposite direction, but he stopped her with a little tap on the shoulder.

She was so freaking weak.

"Wynne."

God, she loved the way he said her name.

"Huh?" she asked, still refusing to look at him. Didn't he realize what she was trying to do here? Couldn't he give her a break and leave her alone? She understood about the engagement, and she felt a little sorry for him that he was probably suffering, too, wishing he hadn't made that promise so long ago. But for both their sakes, he needed to let her be.

If only she could find her tongue so she could tell him that.

"Wynne, I've been looking for you."

"Oh? I've been busy lately. In fact, I really need to go now." She pointed toward the door. "I'm meeting some people. . . ."

He placed two fingers under her chin and lifted it, and she couldn't help it, her eyes lifted, too. Up, up, up they went, her gaze gradually climbing up his body. To his knees, thighs . . . skipped right over the groin . . . his stomach, chest, shoulders, neck. Face. "We need to talk. I have something very important to tell you. Can we go somewhere private?"

"I . . . I . . ."

The door thingy jangled again. Someone coughed. "Wynne. Dierk?"

"Rolf," they both said in unison.

Dierk jerked his hand away.

Wynne took a couple of stumbling footsteps backward. "I was heading to the checkout."

"Excuse me," the store's owner called. "I have to close up in a couple of minutes."

"Sure, sorry." Wynne hurried up to the counter and handed the grimacing woman the book.

"Sorry to rush you." The woman punched the buttons on the cash register. "My son has a doctor's appointment."

"Again, I'm sorry." Wynne handed the woman the gift certificate Dierk had purchased for her. "I lost track of time."

The store owner smiled as she stamped the certificate and handed it back to her. "Thanks for being understanding."

When Wynne turned around, Rolf was waiting by the door and Dierk was nowhere to be seen.

"So there I was, flogging this girl, and she was loving it, and some dude who thought he was a Dom came strolling over and tried to tell me I was doing it wrong!" Kristy busted into a belly laugh. "I mean, ohmygod, I was ready to tell him to wait his turn and I'd show him how wrong I can do it."

Wynne stirred her drink and smiled.

It wasn't easy pretending to be completely riveted by the conversation. Rolf and Kristy were swapping Dom/Domme horror stories and she felt as out of place as a virgin at an orgy. But that wasn't what was making the situation so painful. It was Dierk.

One thing had always made her crazy, no matter who did it. That was coming to her and saying something along the lines of "We need to talk" and then leaving her hanging. Girlfriends, boyfriends, parents, whoever. Those words always set off alarms in her head.

What could he possibly want to talk to her about?

"Wynne, what's wrong?" Kristy gave her shoulder a nudge. "You're in outer space tonight."

Wynne glanced at Rolf. "I ran into Dierk in the bookstore, and he said he needed to tell me something important."

"Ooh, interesting." Kristy turned a pointed look at Rolf. "Any clue what that might be about?"

"No way. My brother doesn't talk about his personal life, not with anyone." His brows dipped. "I'm heading over to Twilight later. I could try to get something from him if you want. I make no promises, though."

Kristy patted his shoulder. "You're a doll. Thanks." She beamed at Wynne. "Rolf'll find out what the deal is. In the meantime, how about we take a walk down the street? This place is borrr-ring. An absolute snooze. I heard about another club a couple of blocks away. Haven't checked it out yet. Wanna go?"

Wynne was not in the mood to scream over loud music and chase Kristy as she weaved through sweaty bodies gyrating on the dance floor. "I don't think so. I'm not the best company tonight. You'd probably have a better time without me."

"Oh, Wynne." Kristy looked genuinely disappointed. She bit her lip and visibly inhaled. "I'm trying here, I really am."

"I know." Wynne gave Kristy an encouraging smile. She glanced at Rolf. He was staring down at his glass, and she couldn't help noticing how quiet he'd become. Now, she felt even worse. Rolf was a nice guy and he had been so happy when she'd agreed to meet him tonight at the bookstore. She was ruining it for him. Or rather, she was letting Dierk ruin it for all of them. "Okay, I'll go. But only if Rolf agrees to go with us."

They both looked at Rolf.

Rolf perked up. "I'd be very glad to accompany you. But I need to settle our tab first."

"We could flag the waitress." Kristy stood and started

searching the increasingly crowded pub. "Wow, when did all these people come in?"

"Don't worry about it." Rolf stood. "I've got to go to the john anyway. I'll take care of it."

As he was swallowed up by the burgeoning throng, Wynne and Kristy both watched him.

"He's a good guy and I can tell he cares for you." Kristy checked her glass then took a couple of swallows.

"Yes, he is. He's a very nice guy. I wish we had chemistry, but it's just not there."

"Not even in the dungeon? You scened with him a couple of times, didn't you?"

"Yes, I did. And I can't say there wasn't any spark. There was when we were scening, but it wasn't the same as when I was with Dierk. Nothing's the same as it is with Dierk. I wish I could stop thinking about him. It sucks so bad. If I let myself, I could totally become a stalker chick to the man. You have no idea how hard it is not to go up to Twilight to try to accidentally run into him. I'm trying to be mature about this, to give him his space and let him have what he wants. But it hurts."

"And it doesn't help when he comes to you." Kristy emptied her glass.

"No, it sure doesn't."

Rolf stepped out of a gathering of tall guys huddled next to their table. "The tab's been paid. Ready to head out, ladies?" He offered each of them a hand, and they both accepted one, and the three of them headed out into the cool evening.

The first chance he got, Dierk was going to kiss his brother.

It wouldn't be much longer. The wait would be over soon, and ohthankgod, Wynne would be his. His heart thumping heavily in his chest, Dierk steered out onto the street, driving toward a local nightclub.

He couldn't tell Wynne there. He'd take her somewhere

quiet and romantic and then he'd beg for her mercy and throw himself at her feet.

In the dungeon, he was her Master, but in all ways, she had bound him, his heart and soul, to her. He belonged to her, and he could not live another day without seeing her, touching her, holding her.

He couldn't get there fast enough, but he somehow managed to obey the speed limit. By the time he pulled into the pub's parking lot, his nerves were so tangled, he wasn't sure he would be able to speak. His hands were literally trembling.

He found an empty spot, maneuvered the vehicle into it, cut off the engine, and ran into the building. Hot air, cigarette smoke, loud music, and people closed in around him. So many people. Everywhere he looked.

Where was she?

He searched the area around the bar then moved out from there, slowly working his way toward the packed dance floor.

There. He caught a glimpse of her hair. He pushed his way through a wall of men and women only to find she was gone. He changed tactics, this time looking for his brother instead. Rolf was taller, easier to spot in a crowd, and he would be with her.

He did a full three-sixty, looking all around him. It was too fucking crowded.

The music changed. A ballad started playing and people left the dance floor in a rush. He saw her then, standing on the fringe of that crush, chatting with her friend, Raven.

His gaze locked to her, he pushed his way toward her, excusing himself as he wended between small groups of men and women.

She saw him just before he reached her. Her eyes widened.

He took her hand in his, that sweet, delicate, beautiful little hand, and kissed every fingertip. How long had he waited for this moment? How many times had he dreamed of it? He pulled her into his arms and kissed her.

If she was shocked, her surprise didn't last long. She wrapped her arms around his neck and kissed him back, and his head started spinning. She tasted delicious. She fit in his arms so perfectly. And she smelled absolutely delectable, and he couldn't get enough of her. Couldn't kiss her long enough. Couldn't hold her closely enough. Couldn't pull her scent in deeply enough.

But even though he was sure he would drop dead if he pulled his lips from hers, he made himself. "Come with me."

Heavy lidded and looking well kissed, she nodded. He started the long walk toward the exit, her hand firmly grasped in his.

Finally they were outside, free of the oppressive stink and noise and crowd.

"What's going on, Dierk?"

"Please, don't make me tell you here. Can you wait just a few minutes? I'd rather go somewhere private."

She nodded and followed him to his car. "Okay. But it had better be minutes. Not hours. Not days and definitely not weeks."

20

Wynne didn't want her heart broken, so she kept telling herself, as she tried to recover from Dierk's bone-melting kiss, that he was not about to tell her he'd broken his engagement. That he couldn't live without her. That he loved her.

Those words, *I love you*. If she heard them, she was sure she'd break into a fit of desperate sobs. Never had she wanted to hear them spoken by anyone as much as him.

Dierk drove fast but safely, the sports car weaving through heavy traffic, carrying them to some unknown destination. He said nothing, just glanced at her every now and then.

What was this all about?

Finally, he drove into a quiet, heavily wooded subdivision full of enormous, well-kept homes. He turned onto a gated drive, and once the gate opened, followed the winding private road, parking in front of a huge house that was bigger and more spectacular than the one that had been converted into the bondage dungeon.

She couldn't imagine why he would bring her to a place like

this. Was this another dungeon? Someone's home? If so, whose?

He cut off the car, opened the door. "Stay here."

She nodded.

He walked around the vehicle to help her out. And then, after taking her hand in his, led her around the side of the mansion to a beautiful garden. A pretty gazebo stood in the center, vines with white flowers cascading over the roof. As they moved closer, the scent of jasmine filled her nose.

Even in this still, tranquil place, she was jittery, her heart thumping hard and fast against her breastbone. "This is a beautiful place. So quiet. Does someone live here?"

"Yes." He didn't release her hand until she was sitting on the bench in the gazebo. When he did, he lowered onto one knee. If she didn't know better, she would swear he was about to . . . propose.

He looked into her eyes. "Wynne, I never thought this time would come, but by a miracle it has and all I can do is hope that you can forgive me for hurting you and give me the chance to make you the happiest woman on earth."

She didn't dare believe, no. He couldn't be . . . he was engaged to another woman. "Dierk, what are you saying?" Tears gathered in her eyes. She lifted her hands to her mouth. They were shaking. Her lips were quivering, too.

"I'm saying I love you. I can't live without you. Not even for a minute, and even though I don't deserve you, I beg you to have mercy and tell me you . . . oh God, Wynne, I can't find the right words."

She swallowed hard, three times. "Are you asking me to marry you?"

"Yes!"

"But what about your fiancée?"

"There isn't a fiancée, at least not right now. If you say yes,

well then . . ." He smiled, and her heart felt like it had quadru-
pled in size.

He loved her! It was too good for her to believe.

And he was asking her to marry him?

He was asking her to marry him!

A sob ripped through her chest. Tears, dammed up for days,
burst from her eyes. She dropped her face in her hands and
tried to stop crying. But she couldn't. She was happy. She was
elated. She was grateful and shocked and God only knew what
else.

"Wynne?"

She threw herself forward into his arms and hid her face in
the crook of his neck.

He loved her! It was true. The heartache was over. She
would be his forever, and he would be hers, and ohgod, this was
the most wonderful, perfect, amazing, beautiful moment of her
life and she didn't want it to end, ever.

She didn't know how long he held her as she cried. His embrace was warm and comforting and eventually she stopped
weeping and snuffling.

"Are you okay?" he asked, looking at her with worry-riddled
eyes.

"I'm better than okay, now." She sniffled.

He wiped a tear away from her eye. "I'm not okay."

Her heart stopped. "Why?"

He smiled. "Because you haven't given me an answer yet."

She laughed. "Yes. Yesyesyesyesyes!"

His smile brightened and he visibly exhaled. He pulled her
into a tight hug, stood, pulling her off her feet, and swung her
round and round until she was dizzy and laughing and begging
for him to stop.

He did, but only to kiss her again until her head was spinning even faster than her body had been and it felt like she wasn't

standing in a garden on earth anymore but floating in heaven, cradled in the arms of a strong, beautiful angel.

"There is one thing I need to tell you, though. Something important." His voice shook a little as he spoke, and her blood chilled, goose bumps prickling at her nape.

"What's wrong?"

"I wish I didn't have to tell you this, because there is nothing I fear more than losing you. But I can't keep the truth from you, not for one more minute."

"Dierk? What is it?" No possibilities popped into her head. Absolutely none. She simply couldn't imagine anything that would be so terrible that she wouldn't want to marry this man. He was strong and gorgeous and devoted and free, now, free to marry her.

"I'm not exactly the man you think I am. I told you that before, but I didn't explain."

"So what does it mean?" Again, she came up with nothing, no idea what he might be talking about. She'd met his brother, so she knew he was who he said he was. He was Dierk Sorenson. The family resemblance was too obvious to be denied.

He helped her back up onto the bench, then sat beside her. And, looking deeply into her eyes, he said, "I'm not mortal. I don't age like a mortal. I've lived for centuries."

What? "That's impossible."

"No, it's very possible."

"You're hundreds of years old?"

His expression dead serious, he nodded. "Yes. I am a *dejenen*. I am what you would call a vampire."

Wynne's heart felt like it had been torn from her body. It ached, and she suddenly couldn't wait to get away from this dark garden with all the shadows and moonlight fast enough. She swallowed a sob and tried to pretend she wasn't about to fall apart. "Um, can you please take me home?"

"Are you okay?"

"Yes, I'm fine. I'm just a little confused and I think I just need some time to . . . absorb all of this. It's a lot to take in all at once." She was going to cry. Hard. Her stomach was clenching as a big sob gathered in her chest again.

This wasn't happening. It was a nightmare. The man she couldn't stop thinking about was finally free to be with her and now he tells her that he thinks he's a vampire.

How cruel was fate, to make such a good, kind, loving man have such a horrible mental illness.

She didn't make it into the car before the tears started flowing again.

Wynne was completely lost, her feelings in such a jumble, she couldn't sort them out. It felt like someone had ripped her insides out, run them over with a Hummer a few times, and then crammed them back inside.

Vampires.

Vampires?

What was she dealing with? A man who was truly insane, or maybe just a little weird? It didn't matter, really . . . did it? She loved him. Loved with a capital L.

Love was a powerful thing, and it could give her strength to . . .

Oh God.

Now lying on the bathroom floor, curled in a fetal position, she sobbed so hard, she dry heaved. She rolled onto her back, the tile chilling her burning skin.

Whywhywhy was this happening?

No matter how she felt about Dierk, how would a relationship with a man who didn't know the difference between reality and fantasy survive? It couldn't.

Her recipe for heartbreak: a dollop of dark good looks, a

dash of sensual domination, blended with a pinch of insanity. In other words, Dierk Sorenson.

Unsteady on legs as rigid as molten marshmallow, Wynne unlocked the bathroom door and stumbled down the hall toward the kitchen. She didn't bother switching on the light. Already, the first twinges of an oncoming migraine were stabbing through her skull. Better to leave all the lights off.

"Wynnie, is that you?" The sleepy voice came from the general direction of the couch.

"Kristy, why are you sleeping in the living room?"

"Because my bed's wet."

After Wynne got a glass of cold water and a couple of Tylenols, she flopped into the chair positioned next to the couch and kicked her feet up onto the coffee table. "Why is your bed wet?" She pulled the afghan off the back of the chair and wrapped it around her shoulders.

"Long story." Kristy yawned. "How was your night? Better than mine, I hope?"

"I doubt it."

Kristy jerked upright. "What? Why?"

Wynne watched her shadowy form lean to one side, and knowing what she was about to do, said, "Please, leave the light off. I have a migraine."

"Okay. Is that why you had a bad time with Dierk?"

"No, not exactly." Wynne didn't bother suppressing the heavy sigh surging up her chest. "Tell me you had no idea Dierk is insane. I mean, certifiable. Because if you say otherwise, I might have to hold it against you."

"Insane? Hell no, I didn't know. What makes you think he's crazy?"

Wynne dragged her hand over her eyes. "He thinks he's a vampire."

"Oh."

Silence.

After a while, Wynne felt an awkward vibe arcing between them. She wondered why Kristy hadn't said another word, hadn't offered any kind of sympathy or support. She found herself trying to hide the hurt under a wave of chatter, "I feel bad for him. He has so much going for him. To be delusional—"

"He isn't."

"A vampire? I know."

"No, he isn't delusional." Kristy leaned forward. "At least, not if what I've heard is true."

What? Her words stung like a slap on the face. Wynne literally gasped. "You've heard rumors about him thinking he's a vampire and you didn't tell me?"

"Nope, I didn't hear rumors. I heard honest-to-God proof, provided by credible witnesses."

"What?"

"I know, it sounds crazy, but—"

"Kristy!"

"Vampires are real. And not only is Dierk a vampire, but so is his brother Rolf."

What was this? She'd never known Kristy to be gullible. Quite the opposite, Kristy was übercynical, almost impossible to convince of anything. "I'm not hearing *you* say that Dierk and Rolf are real-life Draculas. I'm dreaming. No, it's a nightmare."

"Nope, it's not, and I am saying just that." Kristy moved, sitting right beside her. "Think, Wynnie. You've spent some time with both Rolf and Dierk. Have you ever seen either one eat anything?"

That was something she'd noticed. When Dierk had taken her to dinner, she hadn't seen him eat a single bite, but she'd assumed it was because he was nervous. "No."

"Have you seen them during daylight hours?"

Now that one was tough. She had to think some. "Um, no, well, maybe. But most of the time it was dark outside. I assumed that was because they worked during the day, like most normal people do . . . ?"

"Dierk's job is managing the dungeon. The dungeon's hours are from sundown to sunrise," Kristy pointed out.

Wynne pulled the afghan tighter around her shoulders. "Yeah, but I figured that was just a marketing ploy; they're playing with the dungeon's name. That, and I assumed there weren't very many folks interested in coming to a bondage dungeon during the day."

"It's not a ploy. The Sorenson brothers are all vampires, and Twilight is their playground, but it's more than that. It's their hunting territory, too."

So far, she hadn't heard anything convincing. Weird. Bizarre. Startling. But not logical. Not persuasive. "I can't believe you're buying what has to be tall tales and rumors. So far your arguments can be easily and rationally explained."

Kristy gave her a squinty glare. "I can't believe you're so unwilling to be objective and look at the facts." She extended an index finger. "One, neither man eats."

"That we've seen," Wynne interjected. "It doesn't mean they never eat. Oh, and they drink. I've seen them do that much."

"Sure, their bodies can digest a liquid diet. Blood is, after all, a liquid." Kristy added her middle finger. "Two, they don't ever go out during the day. Not for anything."

"Are you sure?"

"Positive."

"No, you're not. Have you ever tried to coax one of them out during the day? I could test Dierk. Tell him I need him to come over right away."

Kristy scowled. "Sure you could do that, but I'm telling you he won't go outside in the sun, not even if you were in danger. Well, maybe if you were in danger he would. But it wouldn't be a good thing." After a beat, she added, "Let's say you staged something, so he was led to believe you were in mortal danger. If he tried to save you, it would kill him—"

"But only if he was a *real vampire*." Wynne dropped her face into her hands and shook her head. "I can't believe I even spoke those words aloud. It can't be. Vampires aren't real. I repeat, vampires do not exist, outside of movie theaters and bookstores."

"Yes, they are. They do. And I know this because"—Kristy extended her ring finger—"three, one of them fed from someone I know personally, and she told me. You need to hear her story. Seriously. Dierk and Rolf Sorenson are honest-to-God vampires. If I can't convince you, she will."

The next night, Kristy jumped up at the sound of someone knocking on their apartment door. "She's here! Wynne, Adeline's here, the woman I told you about."

Wynne, fully expecting to find a very interesting, most likely bizarre individual on the other side of the door, slowly made her way across the living room.

Kristy pulled open the door, hugged the attractive woman at the door, and then stepped to one side. "Adeline, this is my friend Wynne. Thank you for coming."

"It's my pleasure." Adeline, who looked nothing like Wynne expected, with her expensive clothes and dignified demeanor, stepped into the living room.

"Please have a seat." Kristy waved her toward the couch. Once their guest was sitting, Kristy perched on the nearby chair. "I was hoping you might share a certain story with my roommate. I promise, she won't tell anyone."

Adeline met Wynne's gaze and smiled. "You've fallen in love with one of *them*?"

"Dierk Sorenson," Kristy said.

"Dierk." Adeline's smile turned wistful. She was very lovely. "I've heard about him, but never had the pleasure."

"He's everything his reputation suggests." Kristy hopped up. "Something to drink, Adeline?"

Wynne gave them both questioning glances. "What reputation? Kristy, you never mentioned a reputation."

"No, thank you," Adeline answered.

Kristy shrugged, returning to her seat. "I didn't lie to you, Wynne. He's everything I told you." She turned her attention to their visitor. "From what I heard, Dierk's settled down quite a bit lately, because of Wynnie here." Kristy leaned closer. "He's in love with her."

"Oh?" Adeline's meticulously groomed brows shot to the top of her forehead. But just as quickly, and before Wynne could talk herself into serious insult, all signs of shock vanished from her face. "I see now why you might ask me to share my story. "I meant no insult," she said to Wynne. "The *dejenen* don't fall in love easily, especially with a mortal."

Wynne gave a weak smile. "I think Kristy's exaggerating. Love is a very strong word. Lust is probably more appropriate," she lied.

Kristy gave an emphatic shake of the head. She poked an index finger at Wynne. "Don't lie." Then she turned to Adeline. "He told her his secret."

Adeline nodded. "They don't tell anyone about their true nature. Quite the opposite, they go to great lengths to hide it."

"And yet you learned," Wynne pointed out. "If they are so good at hiding their 'true nature,' would you know?"

"There was no way to hide it from me. I was the companion to a *dejenen* for almost three decades, and some things couldn't be hidden from me after some time had passed." She smoothed her hair back from her face and leaned close. "Can you guess my age? Please, don't be afraid you'll insult me. You won't."

Wynne took a look at the woman's face. There were some very faint signs of age, thinning of the skin under her eyes, little crinkles at the corners, a slight indentation between her brows. She guessed the woman was in her mid to late thirties.

Then again, plastic surgeons had a powerful arsenal against the effects of aging these days.

"Before you ask," Adeline offered, "you have my word that I've had no plastic surgery. No lifts, acid peels, fillers, nothing." She chuckled. "If you've seen photos of some of the celebrities these days, you know plastic surgery has its limits."

Doubting her initial guess, Wynne took another long, hard look and decided, despite any lack of evidence, to bump up her guess to forty. "You won't be insulted?"

"Absolutely not."

"Forty."

The woman smiled, slipped her hand into her purse, and pulled out her driver's license. Without saying a word, she handed it to Wynne.

Wynne checked the photograph first then read the age.

That couldn't be right. Either the woman had lied, and made herself about thirty years older than she was (why?!) or she was using someone else's identity.

Adeline's smile was wry. "I can guess what you're thinking, but I have photographs at home that prove that driver's license is mine, and that I am as old as it says."

And I'm supposed to believe you, just because you say so? "This is too bizarre to believe."

"I didn't believe any of it at first either." Adeline smiled. "But after a while, I couldn't deny the truth. My friends were all aging, getting wrinkles, various parts of their anatomies moving south, while I remained young and strong. It's the venom in their bite. If they only bite you once, there isn't much change. But if you get regular "injections," as I liked to call them, you'll age very slowly, if at all. It's a nice perk, though it comes at a price. One does become a little sensitive to the sun." She dug a card and pen out of her purse, wrote something on the back, and handed it to Wynne. "In case you'd like to call me."

Wynne glanced at the card. "Thanks."

"I have to get going. I have an appointment in LA in the morning." The seventy-one-year-old woman, who didn't look a day over thirty, stood, gave Wynne one last smile, and then gave Kristy a hug. "It's good seeing you again."

"You, too. I hope it won't be three years before I see you next."

"It's hard to say. Business has been keeping me busy. But I'll try to get back before too long." She glanced at her wristwatch.

"Good. And congratulations on your new line," Kristy said as she followed Adeline to the door. "Looks like it's doing very well."

"Thank you. I'm quite pleased with it." She waved at Wynne. "Your friend won't be needing my products anytime soon, but I'd be happy to send you some more samples."

Kristy's nod was exuberant. "Oh yes, I'd love that. Thanks."

"I'm very glad to do it. Good-bye, now."

It struck Wynne the moment Adeline had stepped through the door, after she flipped the card over and read it. "That's Adeline Landgre? As in, *the* Adeline Landgre?"

"Sure."

"The Adeline Landgre who owns *Jeunesse éternelle* Cosmetics?"

Kristy grinned. "In case you haven't guessed it by now . . . Her secret formula? Vampire spit. Injections might keep a girl from aging almost entirely, but rubbing a little on the skin works wonders for crow's-feet and laugh lines. No pesky side effects either, like an unnatural sensitivity to the sun, if you get my drift." She winked. "Oh, and for God's sake, don't tell anyone."

"Do you honestly think they'd believe me if I did?"

Kristy gave her an I-told-you-so smile. "It's possible. Not everyone is as closed minded as you."

21

It was here.

And Dierk would be here soon, too.

Wynne was so excited she was practically jumping up and down.

Money was such a small price to pay, even if the volume of money she'd had to gather to buy his gift hadn't been exactly miniscule. It had taken a fairly hefty dose of creativity, a little luck, and the willingness to sacrifice to come up with enough cash to buy Dierk his heart's desire, but she'd done it and she couldn't wait for him to see what she had for him.

She held a 1937 first edition signed copy of Tolkien's *The Hobbit* in her hands. It smelled so good, like an old house with dark secrets. The dust jacket was absolutely perfect, the blue and green colors still vibrant. The inside pages were slightly yellowed but still nicely preserved. This was truly a once-in-a-lifetime find, but then again so was the man who was about to receive it.

Her wonderful, kind, loving, immortal vampire would be here any moment.

Gently, she wrapped the book in the packaging the seller had sent it in and then gift wrapped the box. No sooner did she have the last piece of tape in place when a knock sounded at her door.

She didn't walk to the door, she ran, the box cradled in her arms. She opened the door and shoved the gift into his arms.

"What's this?" he asked, clearly stunned.

She grabbed his arm and pulled, coaxing him into the apartment. "A present."

"For what?"

"For . . . because . . ." She took a deep breath, in, out. "I guess it would be an I'm-sorry gift."

Still looking puzzled, he shook his head. "You have no reason to be sorry."

"Yes, I do. I wasn't exactly open minded when you told me about . . . you being special. And I'm sorry."

"Oh Wynne. You don't need to apologize for that." He cupped her cheek and gazed into her eyes. "I didn't expect you to believe me right away. It's not like I told you this isn't my natural hair color. I was asking you to believe the impossible."

He still hadn't opened the box, dammit. He needed to open it before she tore into it herself.

Wynne pointed at the gift. "Won't you please open it? I'm dying, here."

He visibly sighed. "Okay." He methodically removed each piece of tape, unfolded the wrapping paper, opened the box, and removed the packing as if he was uncovering a priceless artifact in an archeological excavation. It was excruciating to watch. Absolute torture.

He did it on purpose.

But the flash of amazement in his eyes when he finally saw the book was worth every sacrifice, every agonizing minute she'd waited. She felt like her heart was about to explode, she was so happy and excited.

He looked at her as if she were an angel offering him eternal salvation. "Wynne?"

About to cry—she was getting way too weepy these days—she cupped her hands over her mouth and sniffled. "Vampire or not, Dierk, I love you."

He set down the book and swept her into his arms, and oh yes, it felt so good and so right and so natural. He lifted her chin and kissed her until she saw stars and then he kissed her some more, and her mind went totally blank.

All that mattered was this moment and this man. His arms, enfolding her body; his lips, tasting and taking; his tongue, plunging into her mouth and filling it with his sweet flavor; and his body, hard and hot.

She would not, could not, let him go. Not now, not ever. And she was determined to make that perfectly clear by the end of the night.

While he kissed her to oblivion, she slipped her hands into his shirt and stroked the warm, smooth skin she found beneath it. His pecs were hard bulges covered by warm satin, his nipples tight little peaks that grew rigid beneath her fingertips. Eyes closed, and still totally lost in his kisses, she unfastened each button and pushed the shirt down his arms. It finally fell to the floor.

Now, the pants.

She reached for his belt but he caught her hands in his fists and forced them behind her back. Ohhh, yes, how she loved being dominated! She sighed into their joined mouths and then gave a little squeal when he caught her up in his arms.

He carried her with such ease, as if she weighed as little as a child. Across the living room and down the hall he hurried. He stopped at the end. "Which one?"

"There." She pointed at her bedroom door.

"Okay." He gave the door a kick, making it swing open, carried her to the bed, and set her down. His gaze was smoldering hot, and she physically felt it as it swept up and down her body, like the lick of a flame.

"Take me, Dierk. I'm yours." She pulled her shirt off and tossed it aside.

Something dark flashed in his eyes. "Are you sure?"

"Absolutely."

He moved closer, every muscle in his arms, shoulders, and chest tight, rippling and bulging. He looked fierce and dangerous, like a predator stalking its prey, and she couldn't help squirming on the bed, her body so inflamed with need she wanted to cry.

"If we take this step, there's no going back," he warned. "I won't be able to let you go."

"Please, Dierk. I want you. I need you."

His expression softened a tiny bit. "Baby, I need you, too. More than you know." This time, his kiss was soft and sweet; at least, it was for a short time. But as it continued, it grew bolder, more possessive, and she was more than happy for it. Just as she was more than happy to let him gradually strip away the rest of her clothes, one piece at a time.

When she was fully nude, he stopped kissing her, but only long enough to give her one up and down look that sent shudders of need rippling through her body.

"Undress me now." He straightened up, and she scrambled off the bed, eagerly getting to work doing exactly what he'd asked. The shoes came off first, then the socks, belt, pants, underwear.

His body was a work of art, truly. A study in male perfection, from his thick mane of wavy hair to his well-formed feet, and every single inch in between. And his cock . . . It was thick and long and hard and she couldn't wait to feel it gliding in and out of her at last. She'd been denied that pleasure for far too long.

He climbed up on the bed and pulled her onto it with him.

But when she tried to lie down, he stopped her. "No." He reclined back, took his cock in his hand, and gave it a slow swipe up and down. Her mouth filled with saliva. "I have been dreaming of you taking me in your mouth."

"Oh yes, Dierk." She bent over, replaced his hand with hers, gave his thick rod a couple of strokes, and then opened her mouth and pulled the round head inside. He tasted so good, impossibly good. She drew hard, sucking him in deeper, and skimmed her flattened hands up his thick thighs. His leg muscles were hard as concrete beneath her fingertips.

She moaned, relaxed her throat, and took him deeper, and her effort was rewarded with a deep, rumbling groan of raw male need.

This was right. It was perfect. The moment she had dreamed of, hoped for, waited for. *Please, don't let it end.*

Spurred by the sound of Dierk's labored breathing, she settled into a steady rhythm, moving up and down, his cock slipping down her throat and back out again. She stopped every now and then to swirl her tongue round the head like a lollipop. With every stroke, lick, and suck, her own body grew tighter, her need burning hotter.

"Enough." He gently lifted her head, hands cupped around the sides.

When her gaze met his, the fire burning in her body flared brighter. A tear slipped from the corner of her eye, and he sweetly wiped it away.

"I love you," she whispered.

"I love you, too, my beautiful, sweet little slave. Tell me you won't ever take another Master."

"There can be only one Master for this slave, and he's you. I have always belonged to you, and I always will."

He kissed her again and again and again, until she had to drag in little gulps of air and she felt like she would die if that cock wasn't inside her right now.

He forced her onto her back, pushed her knees out, and settled his hips between her thighs, and she smiled up into his eyes, knowing he was about to mark her as his for the rest of her life. His cock pushed at her entry. It slipped inside and surged deep, and her back tightened, arching. Stars exploded behind her closed eyelids.

So full. He fit her perfectly.

She looked up, reached for him, but he wove his fingers between hers and pressed her hands back down, pinning them to the mattress. He slid his hips back, withdrawing almost entirely, then slammed them forward.

Oh the agony and ecstasy, both.

There were no ropes or chains or leather cuffs. There were no benches or crosses or tables. It didn't matter. They weren't needed. He had her submission, her surrender. She gladly relinquished all she was and all she had to him. Her decadent lover. Her Master. Her everything.

And he accepted her offering with clear appreciation. They had an understanding without needing to write out a list of rules. There was no need for safe words or limits.

They were one, in mind.

Their bodies worked as one, his strong, hard form and her softer one. They withdrew and met in a rhythm that met the thrumming need pulsing through their beings.

They were one, in body.

And as their need built, they touched and caressed each other, sharing the emotions they had been forced to stifle for so long. There were no words exchanged: there was no need for words. Their energies swirled and churned, coursing through Dierk's body before charging through Wynne's. She was his and he was hers. She was him. He was her.

They were one, in spirit.

When they reached climax, they soared over the crest together. The energy pulsing through them increased a hundred times. It tingled and buzzed and zapped through every cell in Wynne's body as she shuddered. She had never felt so powerful, so alive or strong.

She laughed and cried and clung to Dierk's sweat-slicked body as he surged forward, giving one final thrust. And then spent, he kissed her face, her shoulders, her hair, rolled off of her, and pulled her into his arms.

"Ohmygod," she said, feeling like she'd just done the world's best drug. Her head was spinning. Her body was twitching all over. And she still felt like she was strong enough to pick up a small car and toss it. "Ohmygod, ohmygod, ohmygod."

Dierk gave her a pat. "You thought that was something. We're just getting started."

Smiling, she took his hand and placed it between her legs. "I was hoping you were going to say that."

22

Dierk couldn't recall the last time he felt like this, like the rest of his life was hinged on the outcome of one critical moment, a decision that wasn't his to make.

He knew his brother Shadow loved him.

He knew Shadow wished to see him happy.

But he also knew Shadow was bound by a law that had been set in place eons ago, one that had a purpose.

If the king gave anyone permission to step beyond the law, he could face the worst consequences.

That couldn't happen. Much more than one man's happiness was at stake. The stability of a kingdom, for one.

Dierk hesitated. He shouldn't be here. Shouldn't be asking this favor, and he wouldn't if he had possessed the strength to deny Wynne her greatest wish. He loved her too much not to try.

No, he loved her too much to fail. He would pay any price to make her his forever.

"His Majesty will you see now," the king's secretary repeated, standing at the open door to His Majesty's private office.

"Thank you." Dierk dragged his sweaty palms down the sides of his legs, lifted his chin and, ignoring the heavy pounding of his heart, entered the room. As expected, his brother was sitting at his desk, his head lowered, reading a piece of paper he held in his hands. Dierk stopped just inside the room and waited for his brother to wave him over.

It took what felt like an eternity for the king to lift his head. "My brother." Shadow motioned, welcoming Dierk with a smile. "I've been wanting to speak with you." He stood, motioning toward a set of chairs sitting in front of the empty fireplace. "Come, tell me how things are going. I've grown weary of heavy political issues."

"I wish I could tell you I've come to amuse you, brother, but I'm afraid it's for a much more weighty matter."

"Oh really?" The king sat, crossed an ankle over his knee. "What matter is that?"

Dierk sat, mirroring his brother's position. "I need to speak about the Joining."

His brother's eyebrows lifted. "Continue."

"I understand it's against the law for any man but the king to pursue the Joining with a mortal woman. But I find myself here, prepared to beg, to grovel, for permission to do just that."

His brother chuckled. "Isn't it amusing how something so small and seemingly powerless can cut us down?"

"It is."

The king's eyes glittered with laughter. "My enemies can't destroy me—though they've tried—but one unkind look from my wife would devastate me. She weighs less than our dog, possesses not an ounce of cruelty, and submits to my every wish, and still I am utterly captivated by her."

Dierk could easily relate to his brother in that regard. "I feel the same way."

"When a man loves a woman so thoroughly, he cannot live another moment not knowing she is his, she will always be his."

"Yes. The thought of losing Wynne makes me sick."

His brother leaned forward and rested a hand on Dierk's knee. "The law is clear. You can't Join with her. I know you're aware of that."

"Yes." Dierk felt all hope slipping away. "I know, but I was wondering . . ."

"What? That I would grant you permission to break the law?" He removed his hand. "You know what price I would pay if I did that. And our people, what price they would pay, too."

"Of course."

The king tipped his head. "Still, you asked?"

"I have no choice. I love her."

His brother stood, arms crossed over his chest. "What's wrong with just marrying her?"

As required, Dierk stood, despite the fact that his legs were so shaky he wondered if they would hold his weight. "Nothing."

"Yet you ask for more. You ask for the impossible."

"I've found the impossible. You know how that feels, how desperate this kind of all-consuming love makes a man. I can't think of anything but Wynne. I've tried. I feel incomplete without her."

"If you are married, you will be connected in all ways but one, as so many have done before you. It was enough for them. Why isn't it good enough for you?"

"But you know how painful and frustrating it will be, for both me and Wynne. To deny what we need is cruel."

"To allow you to Join with Wynne is to sign my own fate." The king sighed. "The law was written to protect us all. It is the one law that even a king is charged to uphold, or face the punishment of death."

Shaking his head, Dierk closed his eyes. "I made a mistake, coming to you. I should have gone through with it without asking your permission. At least then—"

"I would have been forced to live with the guilt of having to sign your order of execution."

Dierk shrugged. "It seems you won't be able to avoid it."

"Then you'll Join with her anyway, even if I deny your request?" His brother dropped his head, shoved his fingers through his hair. "At least give me some time to look into the options."

"There is no time. Tomorrow is the full moon. I won't wait. I can't wait. Not even a month."

His brother's expression was grim. "Then I have no choice...."

Assuming the conversation was over, Dierk backed toward the exit. Knowing he would soon pay the price for following his heart, he had only one thought. He would spend every minute he had left with the woman he loved.

Not doubting for one moment what he was about to do, Dierk took Wynne's hands in his the next night and said the words of the Joining in the Ancient Tongue.

They had spent the past twenty-four hours talking about this moment, what it meant for them and what would happen afterward. Because they were likely to lose their lives, Dierk kept his wishes to himself as they discussed the ritual. He wanted Wynne to make this decision freely, without feeling any pressure from him. Instead of telling her how badly he longed to Join with her, he tried to stick to the basic facts about the Joining—specifically, how it would bind them spiritually. If one died, the other died. Their energies would blend. And during the most intimate moments, they would sense what the other did: hear what they heard, feel what they felt, taste what they tasted.

Wynne stood before him motionless now, the light of the full moon reflecting off her hair and making her look like an angel. The scent of jasmine was heavy in the cool air, the white petals overhead gleaming silver.

This was the perfect place. The perfect time. The perfect woman.

He accepted the choker from his brother Rolf and lifted it to Wynne's neck.

It was almost done. She would soon be his forever, her soul a part of him, filling the cold, empty hollow inside. He secured the clasp at her nape and brushed his knuckles along her cheekbone. His forever.

His gaze locked to hers, he mentally reached for her. She might not hear his voice clearly yet, but she would feel his presence. He sent her loving thoughts.

You are mine and I am yours. Forever.

"Almost done," Dierk said aloud. "I promise to make you the happiest woman in the world, for the rest of your life." The need to complete the Joining was an excruciating ache now. Trembling, he spoke the rest of the words of the ritual, but the overwhelming urge to complete the final steps grew more intense with each sentence he uttered. By the time he had completed the Promise, he was so weak, he could barely stand, his limbs heavy, his heart hard and cold.

Almost done.

He tipped his head, closed his eyes, and whispered, "Ask me to kiss you."

"Kiss me, please!" Wynne threw her arms around his neck and pressed her lips against his. An electrical charge jumped between their joined mouths. She parted her lips and he slipped his tongue inside. The energy zapped along his tongue, then charged through his body, blazing down his nerves. Heat gathered deep inside his chest, scorching, and yet not painful. The ice that had encased his frozen heart melted away and joy swelled inside until tears gathered in his eyes.

The Joining was almost finished. He was nearly whole.

He couldn't wait. The final step was next: a bite, like so many he had enjoyed before and yet different. This one was a promise. A claiming. And a surrender. More than a kiss sealing marriage vows, this bite would bond them forever. He needed to complete the Joining before the magnificent fullness left him and he was empty again. He couldn't bear to think of existing another minute without Wynne's glorious soul filling him.

His fangs extended. He dragged his tongue down her throat. Her skin was sweet, salty, delicious.

"Now, my love," he murmured, pulling Wynne flush against him. "Are you ready?"

"Yes," she said on a sigh. "Yes, now. Please."

His fangs pierced her skin and his mouth filled with the decadent flavor of her blood.

"Yessss." She clawed at his shoulders, stiffened against him as he eagerly drank from her. With each swallow, a different kind of burning sparked inside him, desperate carnal need. He wanted her like he had never wanted a woman before. His cock surged to a throbbing erection. He roughly yanked her closer and pushed his knee between her legs. As his venom took hold of her, she writhed against him, grinding her pussy against his thigh, stirring his lust to even greater heights.

He whispered her name against her neck, repeated it over and over. It was the most glorious name he'd ever spoken. Each time he said it, he soared closer, closer to orgasm. And then she groaned and shuddered against him as a climax overtook them both.

It was done.

His precious Wynne belonged to him forever. He swept her

into his arms and looked down into her heavy-lidded gaze. "My love for you will have no end. We will be together forever, no matter what happens to us now."

Movement in the distance caught his eye. A man. Running.

Dierk's joy faded, but only slightly. He had hoped his brother would wait a little while before sending guards to have him arrested.

He tightened his hold on Wynne.

"What's wrong?" she asked, still not seeing the man heading their way.

"We're about to pay the price for our love." He motioned toward the approaching man, knowing she couldn't see him yet. "Remember, we talked about this. Someone is coming to arrest me now."

"No!" Wynne sobbed, twisted, and arched her back, forcing him to set her down.

"My sweet Wynne." He pulled her into an embrace but she fought out of it. "Please don't get upset. We knew this would happen."

"I don't give a damn. I won't let anyone arrest you," she murmured, sounding surprisingly calm. Her expression was fierce, determined, damn sexy. "Nobody is going to make you pay anything. We've done nothing wrong."

"It's Shadow," Rolf said.

Rolf was right. It was their brother, the king.

"Am I too late?" Glowering, Shadow stopped directly in front of Dierk. "Did you defy me?"

Dierk gently tried to force Wynne behind him. "I did."

"Dammit," Shadow spat. "You ass."

"*You're* an ass." Jumping forward, Wynne poked the king in the chest. Dierk grabbed her wrists and yanked them behind her back, but as he struggled to gather both into one of his fists, she growled, "What gives you the right to deny anyone the happiness they deserve?"

"Wynne, stop. He is my king. Your king." Dierk tried to get her to turn around and look at him, but she wasn't going to let that happen without putting up a good fight. And thanks to the strength she'd gained through the Joining, she was giving him a run for his money.

"I don't give a damn what his title is. He's still an asshole, and I'm not afraid to tell him that." Standing tall, she glared up at his brother, who towered over her. "There's a time and a place for obedience, submission. And maybe you all expect me to shut up and be the good little submissive girl I've become in the dungeon, but I can't. Not when such a gross injustice is about to be done. Love cannot be stopped. It overcomes obstacles or it barrels through them, but either way it wins out over everything else. And our love led us to this place, against your wishes, against your law. We couldn't stop it any more than we could have stopped a typhoon. So, why should we be penalized—"

"I understand." The king crossed his arms over his chest. Wynne snapped her mouth shut. "But the law is clear. Only the king may Join with his bride."

"The law isn't fair—"

Shadow lifted a hand, silencing the fiery little Wynne. "The law has a purpose, and as king I am bound to honor it and every other written in our books."

"Which is your way of telling us you can't do anything to help us," she snapped.

"Oh yes, I can." Shadow nodded. "I have spent the past twenty-four hours looking into this dilemma and I have discovered we have a few options." He extended his index finger. "I can have you arrested and tried for treason and if you are convicted, you will be executed."

"I hope he's got something better than that," Wynne muttered.

"He does. I hope." Dierk braced for what he hoped might be good news.

Shadow extended his middle finger, adding it to the index. "Two, I can step in your place, admit I gave you permission to Join, and pay the consequences for breaking the law."

"I won't let you do that," Dierk said.

"Or three." The king extended his ring finger. "You can confess your guilt now, relinquish your right to a trial, and place yourself at my mercy."

Dierk briefly considered all three and quickly concluded there was only one that gave them any hope whatsoever.

Ironically, he was now forced to do what he'd asked Wynne to do all along. He had to place his trust at another man's feet, and blindly have faith that it wouldn't be crushed.

He released one of Wynne's wrists, dropped on one knee, and nodded to her, suggesting she do the same.

She hesitated but complied.

He said, "Before this witness, we confess we knowingly and freely broke the law, completed the Joining against your counsel and in secret, and beg for your mercy, Your Grace."

"You made a wise choice." Shadow paused. "It pains me to do this, but I must find you guilty of Treason."

Dierk felt Wynne's hand tremble. He gave it a gentle squeeze.

"Your sentence is that you will be banished until my anger is appeased. You will spend this time overseeing the reconstruction of our castle in Ljubljana."

"Ljubljana?" Wynne whispered.

Trying to hide his jubilation, Dierk fought a grin. "Yes, My King. Thank you, Your Grace." He watched as Shadow took a step backward.

That was it? He would go to Slovenia and oversee the rebuilding of the castle that was destroyed? That was no punishment. Hell, it was a reward!

"Ljubljana?" Wynne repeated.

He didn't move until his brother was out of sight, then he leapt to his feet, hauled Wynne off the ground, and swung her in a wide circle. "Get ready, Sweetheart. We've been banished to the most beautiful place on earth."

She squealed and giggled in that delightful way that had him smoldering.

Rolf clapped him on the back. "Congratulations!"

He turned to Rolf. "Thank you. For everything."

After they shared a hearty hug, Rolf said, "It makes me happy seeing the two of you together."

"You'll find her someday, too," Dierk said, "the woman you can't live without. God help you when you do." After giving Rolf another quick hug, he headed toward the house. He had a lot to look forward to, the least of which was taking home his Joined mate, his wife, and making love to her until neither of them could lift an eyelid.

This was too wonderful to be true. Not only was she married to the man of her dreams but she was lucky enough to enjoy a much deeper and more intimate bond with him. He was her Master. He was her husband. Her lover. Her partner. And, in the most literal sense, her soul mate. A piece of her belonged to him now, inhabited him, literally. Their fates were tied to each other, and she would have it no other way.

Now, when she gazed into Dierk's eyes, she no longer saw dark shadows, secrets, sorrow, and regret, but hope, love, and joy.

It was time.

In their bedroom, she knelt before him, the oiled hemp rope she'd taken from his cabinet lying on the floor in front of her. More than anything, she wanted to feel his rope binding her, holding her tightly. A loving web, caressing, grazing, chafing.

"Please, Master. I've waited a long time for this."

Dierk stood, went to her, cupped her chin, and brushed his lips over hers, a teasing, tempting kiss. "I couldn't deny you anything. It may be me tying the knots around you, but you have bound me to your soul."

He picked up the rope and stepped around her back. His breath caressed her nape, making her shiver. He leaned close and the heat from his body added tingles to the shivers. He eased a hand around her side and she closed her eyes and sighed.

He dragged the rope around her chest, just under the swell of her breasts. "Close your eyes, my love. Feel my caress."

Wynne concentrated on her breathing as Dierk tied knot after knot around her torso, encasing her in a web of rope. As the web tightened, she began to feel an odd sensation, like she was floating. The soft ropes grazed her skin. It was so good. A patient, slow, and gentle seduction.

The rope between her legs shifted, rubbing against her pussy. She inhaled deeply . . . and sighed.

Dierk tied a few more knots down the center of her stomach, making her feel more helpless, powerless. But she wasn't frightened, not when she knew Dierk had control. She heard him speaking. Her love. Her Master. Whispering in her head. "Surrender," he said. "Let go."

Yes, that was what she wanted to do, needed to do.

As he worked, more rope slid across her skin, the knots pressing against her breastbone, her stomach, her mound, and she felt some kind of energy zapping deep inside her. His voice grew louder. "Surrender, Wynne. Give me everything." His words sent tingling vibrations through her body. It felt like a current of electricity was charging through her system. Up to her scalp and back down through her center, down her legs, her feet.

She opened her eyes and saw a faint light connecting her to her Master. It was rotating between them, joining them.

Confused, she started to pull back and fight his voice, trying to control the energy, to keep it inside. But the power of his words was too strong. It pulled her back under, like an overpowering surge of water, a wild tempest. She was lost but it was okay. Better than okay.

There were two energy streams now, their blended energies, pushing through her body, from her feet to her head. Out it rushed, into the head of her Master, down through his body, and back to her. It was magical. It was beyond words. Exquisite. Beautiful. Rare and precious. They were connected so intimately now that he didn't have to touch her for her to feel his touch. All he had to do was think it.

She heard herself sigh again, but through Dierk's ears this time, as if she was inside Dierk's body and he in hers. Her reward was so close now, and yet she resisted its pull, wanting this moment to last. Her body was thrumming with sensual energy, her pussy ready to pulse with a hard climax. The churning was gathering force, like a storm cloud, a typhoon. She could come. Release was right there. And yet she held back, living this moment to its fullest. She had never been more energized and alive as now. She was one with Dierk, body, mind, and soul.

Pulsing heat slowly rippled out from her center, the sensation too wonderful for words or even thoughts.

"Sparrow," he said.

She struggled. She fought. One more second, only one.

She lost.

An inferno swept through her body, and her pussy convulsed around aching emptiness. Muscles from her head to the soles of her feet spasmed as ecstasy charged along her nerves like jolts of electricity. She felt like she was racing to the stars, hurled through space. On and on the ecstasy continued through an eternity of unspeakable bliss. She soared to an impossibly beautiful place, hovered there for a short time, and slowly, gradually sank.

He was calling to her, coaxing her back.

When she opened her eyes, she was no longer bound in ropes. And Dierk was kneeling, cradling her in his arms, tears of joy trickling from his eyes.

"That was beautiful," he whispered.

She took his hand in hers and kissed his palm, his fingertips, his wrist. "Thank you. For being my life. My love. My every-thing." She placed his hand between her legs. "Make love to me now. Please. Not like a Master but a man. A husband."

While kissing her to heaven and back, he carried her to the bed and set her down. She returned every stroke and stab of the tongue with one of her own as she scooted toward the center of the mattress, Dierk crawling on hands and knees over her. When she stopped her slow but steady progress, he wedged his hips between her thighs and settled on top of her. He cradled her head in his hands, lifting it and tipping it, deepening the kiss.

He tasted so good, felt even better. How grateful she was right now, having him here with her, touching her at last, kiss-ing her. Finally, they were free to express their feelings, and she was so overcome she started to cry. Little sobs slipped up her throat, only to be swallowed by her husband.

He moved lower, kissing her neck, her collarbone, her breast. He flicked his tongue over her nipple, and little currents of pleasure zinged through her body.

Her pussy was hot, so hot. Wet. *Empty.* She didn't want to wait any longer; the orgasm she'd enjoyed as she was bound was like the most intense foreplay she'd ever experienced. She could think of nothing but taking him deep, of their bodies joining like their spirits had moments ago.

She whimpered, reached down and stroked his thick rod. His skin was smooth as satin, sheathing granite. Warm and alive and perfect. He groaned, gave her nipple a little nip that made her shudder and kissed a warm, wet path to her clenching pussy.

Oh no. She wanted his cock. "No more . . ."

"Impatient, my precious?"

"Yes. And I'm not ashamed to admit it." She tried for his cock again, but he had moved out of her reach, and he wasn't letting her sit up. He pressed one hand to her breastbone, forcing her to lie back down. He lowered his head.

Oh no, he was going to . . .

The first swipe of his tongue nearly sent her to the moon. The second one had her writhing beneath him, caught up in an inferno of need. And the third sent a plea for mercy flying from her lips.

"Please, please," she begged. She curled her fingers into his hair and pulled but he didn't let up. He parted her labia and licked her hard pearl until she was quaking, on the verge of orgasm. "Dierkkkkkk . . ." She arched her back and parted her legs wider, but that did nothing to ease her torment.

Hard, thick cock. That was what she needed. Now. Right now. Not a second from now. Not a fraction of a second from now.

"Now," she yelled. "Now!"

He chuckled. If she hadn't been burning alive, she would have punched him. Hard. Instead, she grabbed his hair and pulled. This time, he moved, crawling up her body until his groin was pressed against hers. "Is this what you want?" He ground that thick rod against her pulsing clit.

"Yes," she whispered between clenched teeth. "Deep. Fuck me."

He lifted her knees, found her entrance, and surged inside.
She saw stars.

Her body coiled into one tight knot.

An inferno whipped through her body.

Then he started moving inside her and their bodies worked
as one, meeting and retreating in a beautiful dance. She felt their
energies blending again and that wonderful sensation whirled
through her system once more. But this time, she wasn't alone,
swooping and soaring on a sparkling current of energy. Dierk
was there with her, and they could see, hear, feel, and think what
the other did. Their thoughts blended, their needs merged, their
wishes and fears melded until there was no separation, only
union.

In this state, they found completion and an ecstasy that
couldn't be imagined. Their combined orgasm was more powerful than anything Wynne had ever experienced, more beautiful and furious than any force of nature she'd seen—tornado,
tidal wave, hurricane, volcano.

And the peace afterward, the contentment and joy—heav-
enly.

She had no idea who or what was responsible for their finding each other, and for all the pieces falling into place as they
had, but she knew she would always be grateful.

She realized her whole life, both the heartache and the happiness, had led her to this point, to this man. To this moment. If
she had missed a turn, if John hadn't dumped her for a cross-
dressing Dom or if Kristy hadn't dragged her to Twilight,
would they have found each other? Would she have lost out on
knowing the perfect, unparalleled joy of total submission?

Someday, she would thank John for forcing her out of her
imaginary world where they were in love and everything was
perfect.

But in the meantime, she had a Dom to please. And please him, she would. In as many ways as she could.

Thanks to her experiences at Twilight, she had a whole new understanding of herself. But more than anything, now she knew a kind of loving that went beyond the ordinary. Sex was no longer a joining of two bodies; it was a joining of two spirits.

Turn the page
for a tantalizing preview
of Kate Pearce's novella in
SOME LIKE IT ROUGH!

On sale now!

"Well, hell."

Luke Warner leaned back and squinted up at the hole in the ceiling, certain he could see the blue sky beyond. He sure had his work cut out for him, but that was what he'd wanted, right? Something to do with his hands, something to connect him to his past. He grimaced as his gaze swept the broken countertops and shelves, the holes in the floor, the leaking pipes.

The old Warner family drugstore on the corner of Keystone and Main in Gulch Town, California, had definitely seen better days. For some reason, he decided it was his job to put it right. It smelled of dirt and mildew now, but once, the store had its own distinct odor of popcorn, coffee, and candy. Luke remembered sitting on a high stool watching his grandpa weigh a handful of pills on the old scales, the way he'd wrapped them in brown paper, the clunking ring of the manual cash register.

His father hadn't wanted to run the shop, and it had been left to rot until Luke had shown up and demanded the key from his perplexed Aunt Josie. With a sigh, he picked up his sleeping bag and rucksack and walked to the back of the store.

There was one room with a door that still locked and an outside toilet with running water and a sink. That would have to do until he got himself fixed up.

He laid out his sleeping bag, stretched out on it, and kicked off his dusty boots. It was a small town. It wouldn't take long for folks to hear he was back. He smiled into the gathering shadows. What would Paul and Julia do then?

Paul let himself in through the back door of Julia's small condo and found her in the kitchen stirring something that smelled like chicken on the stove. He came up behind her and planted a kiss on the back of her neck. She squeaked, and he wrapped his arms around her hips and nuzzled her throat. Strands of her silky brown hair tickled his face. She dropped the spoon into the pan and swung around to face him.

"Don't you ever knock?"

He touched the brim of his Stetson. "No, ma'am, I was brought up in a barn, remember?"

She leaned back against the countertop, her blue eyes serious, her normally laughing mouth a worried line. "That joke is getting old."

"Yeah, I reckon I've been making that one since kindergarten." He raised his eyebrows at her. "So, what's up? You seemed kind of jittery when you called."

"I just spoke to Roxanne. She says Luke is back in town."

Paul blinked at her. "Our Luke?"

Well, he's scarely 'ours' anymore, is he? We haven't seen or heard from him in ten years. But Luke Warner is definitely here."

Paul studied Julia's flushed face. "And?"

"And what?"

"What do you want to do about it?"

"About Luke?" She shrugged, and one of the thin straps of

her blue camisole fell down from her shoulder. He noticed she had no bra underneath. "I don't know."

Paul stepped closer until his large body was only inches away from Julia's. Her nipples tightened through the thin cotton of her cami, and her breathing hitched. He put his hands on her waist and set her on the tiled countertop, reaching over to turn off whatever was cooking on the stove.

"You want to see him, don't you?"

She looked up at him, and he bent his head and licked a slow, lascivious line along the seam of her lips.

"He'll be hard to miss in a town as small as this."

"That's not an answer." Paul slid a hand under her camisole and cupped her right breast, used his finger and thumb to twist her nipple to a hard, needy point. She sighed and shoved her hand into his hair, wiggled closer to the edge of the counter, until her sex rode the thick ridge of his cock in his jeans.

"You want to see him up close and personal, right?" He murmured between kisses and nips. He went still when she caged his face in her hands.

"Don't you want to know why he left?"

"Of course I do, but . . ."

She smiled at him and unbuckled his belt and straining fly. "But, you're worried I'll run off with him?" She wrapped her hand around his cock and squeezed hard, just the way he liked.

"Yeah," he admitted, as she pulled down her shorts with one hand and let them fall to the floor. "You always liked him best."

His fingers plucked at her clit and then slid into the thick wetness of her pussy. He took her hand away from his cock and shoved himself deep into her slick heat, held still as she shuddered around him. Sometimes he liked it like this, hard and fast, Julia having to catch up, giving him every orgasm right around his thrusting shaft rather than against his fingers or mouth.

Tonight he wanted to fuck her hard, as if he could somehow

slow down time and make her realize she didn't want to go anywhere near Luke Warner, that she wanted only him. She cried out and her pussy clenched around his cock. Paul kept slamming into her and only climaxed when she came again, squeezing every last drop of cum out of his balls.

She stroked the back of his neck, her fingers soft. "I don't like him best. I like you. You stayed, remember?"

He lifted his head to stare at her. "I had no choice. I couldn't go off and leave the ranch, now, could I?"

"My hero."

She smiled at him, and he had to smile back. "I don't mind if you see Luke, honey. I'd like to see him myself."

"You would?" Julia studied him and then her gray eyes narrowed. "Not if you're going to beat him up, Paul."

"I wouldn't do that." He pulled out of her and handed her his handkerchief to clean up. "I'd sure appreciate an explanation though. He was my best friend, too. We did everything together, had our first smoke, our first beer, our first mutual jerk off . . ."

"Your first fuck."

Paul kissed her nose. "I prefer to think we were making love to you. It was so fucking sweet. *You* were so fucking sweet to let us."

Julia slipped down from the countertop and pulled her shorts back on. Her slow, dreamy smile indicated that she was as caught up in the past as he was. "If it was so sweet, why did Luke skip town right after?"

Paul tucked his cock back into his boxers and zipped up his jeans. "I don't know. That's one of the reasons I want to talk to him."

Julia washed her hands and turned back to the stove. "I hear he's staying at the old drugstore on Main."

"That wreck? Why the hell isn't he bunking with his aunt? Maybe he's out of money and came back because he had no choice." Paul sat down at the table and stared at the stove expectantly. It was a five-mile drive back to his ranch, and he already knew he had nothing but beer and beef in his refrigerator. If he was staying over, and after Julia's call, he'd had no choice but to turn around and come see her, he loved getting fed as well as fucked.

"I have no idea, but perhaps we should drop by tomorrow and see how he's doing?"

Paul grinned at her. "Yeah, perhaps we should."

"Paul?"

"Yeah, honey?" Paul croaked and opened his eyes to find Julia propped up on her elbows looking down at him, her breasts grazing his chest, her long legs straddling his hips. He had no idea what time it was, only that he was in her bed and that it was still dark. Despite the fact that they'd already made love twice, his cock stirred against her wet, warm sex.

"That question you asked me. The one I didn't want to answer?" Julia kissed his forehead. "You're right. I would like to get up close to Luke again."

Paul carefully lifted her off him and rolled onto his side. He tried to sound casual, even though he knew she wouldn't buy it. "So, do you want me to stay out of the way at the ranch while you fuck him?"

"Why would you do that?"

He shrugged and tried to smile. "Because I'm trying to be the better person, here. I'm trying to give you choices."

"That's not like you at all."

"I know." Hell, it was the hardest thing he'd ever contemplated, giving Julia up, especially to Luke Warner.

She reached out and touched his chest, stroked her fingers over his nipples. "I kind of thought you'd like to be there, too."

He studied her carefully in the dim light. "When you say 'there' do you mean like, physically there?"

"Yes."

His cock reacted quicker than his brain, showed its appreciation of the idea by filling out hard and fast. In the beginning it had always been the three of them and they'd learned about sex together. Somehow, it had felt right and he couldn't shake the notion that it would always feel right. "Like, both of us?"

"That depends on Luke, doesn't it?" Julia's tentative smile cut through the darkness. "I always think of us as a threesome, don't you? Or does that make me some kind of voracious slut?"

"Not in my book, honey." He rolled on top of her and drove his cock deep, felt her curl her arms and legs around him and hold him tight. "I'm happy to do whatever you want as long as I'm part of it."

She lifted her hips into his thrusts and he kept on pumping, slid his hand between them to finger her clit and bring her off with him. He couldn't contemplate sharing Julia with any other man but Luke, and, to be fair, she'd never expressed an interest in fucking anyone else. And, as far as anyone knew, they'd been a couple since high school. The least he could do was give them all a chance to explore every aspect of their old relationship. That was only fair. He groaned as his cum exploded into Julia. Sex with Julia was always excellent; with Luke involved, it might be awesome.

Julia sipped her second cup of coffee and squinted into the sunlight filtering through the blinds of her small kitchen. Paul had gotten up early and gone home to his ranch. Since his parents had decided to retire to Florida, he never had the luxury of walking away from it completely. Despite having some staff to help out, something always required attention, even if it was as dull as repairing fence line or doing the accounts.

When it got really busy out there, during cattle drives, birthing or branding, Julia often went out and stayed with him. She half-smiled. Otherwise she would never see him. And she liked seeing him. Liked the way he used his big, strong, body too . . .

With a sigh, she got off the stool and picked up her briefcase. Time to get to work and face another day of exciting fiscal challenges at the one and only bank in Gulch Town. Not that much ever happened. The most exciting thing this year was when Mr. Murphy's crazy sheepdog had gotten loose and chewed up a load of paperwork and a couple of chairs.

She'd been beyond excited to become assistant manager because it meant she could stay in her hometown, but it also meant she had to deal with Mr. Glynn, the complete asshole who ran the bank and was slowly driving her nuts. Unfortunately he had at least four years before he was due to retire, so unless she wanted to move jobs, or be sent to prison for murder, she was stuck with him. And she'd never wanted to leave, had she? With an ever-changing cast of stepfathers, her only security had come from Paul, Luke, and Gulch Town.

As she walked to her car, she wondered how Luke was doing. How on earth was he going to survive in that wrecked old store his family had abandoned years ago? She knew that several offers had been made to the family to buy up the prime retail space, but they'd all been refused. Had Luke intended to come back all along? Had he been the one behind the family decision not to sell?

On that tantalizing thought, Julia got into her car and drove the five minutes to work. If Luke was moving back, surely he'd need funds? And, as Mr. Glynn preferred golf to sitting behind his desk, she was nominally in charge of the only bank in town. It looked like she might be seeing Luke even sooner than she had anticipated.